KATHLEEN KELLY

Man Trouble
Clubhouse Women Book One

Kathleen Kelly

Disclaimer: The material in this book contains graphic language and sexual content and is intended for mature audiences, ages 18 and older.

ISBN: 978-1922883049

Editing by Swish Design & Editing
Proofreading by Swish Design & Editing
Book design by Swish Design & Editing
Cover design by CT Cover Creations
Cover image Copyright 2023
First Edition 2023

DEDICATION

To the readers and authors who love MC Romance.
Where would I be without you all?

I say this all the time:

Book people are the best people. :)

PROLOGUE

Grim stands outside the bar. He's so confident in his surroundings he doesn't see me lurking in the darkness. Red, his VP, lightly punches him in the arm, and as I've seen him do a thousand times, he pulls out his gun, releases the magazine, makes sure there's one in the chamber, and slams the magazine back into his Glock.

It's his habit. The only one he appears to have, apart from pretty blondes. Even now, one of the whores from the bar walks toward him, throwing her long blonde hair over one shoulder and licking her lips. Grim doesn't have an old lady, but he has a type. This, along with his habit, I can exploit.

Retreating further into the shadows, I jog back to my bike, turn it on, and disappear into the night. I've wanted Grim dead for a long time, but my president has made it clear I am not allowed to start a war. To appease myself, I've been watching him, looking for a chink in his armor. Soon, we will all be playing nice and under one roof. I just need a pretty little thing to help execute my plan, and as it happens, my ex, a stuck-up little princess, will help me, and she won't even know it.

I'm stopped at a light and pull out my cell phone.

Me: *Hey gorgeous, want to go for a ride?*

In response, I get an emoji of the middle finger. Chuckling, I tuck my phone back into my jacket. Elora will come around.

Women are all the same.

First, you fuck up, then you apologize.

They forgive you, and you need to be more careful the next time so you don't get caught.

Elora didn't give me the opportunity to apologize, but she will. The weaker sex always buckles, and she's female, so it's only a matter of time.

Arriving home, I enter my house and go straight to the basement. Here is where I practice my best work. On the wooden bench, I have a Glock 31 in pieces. It holds fifteen .357 bullets and is Grim's weapon of choice. The only working component I'm interested in is the magazine. It wasn't easy, but I removed five bullets and inserted a small syringe inside. When he releases the magazine and slams it back into the gun, it should set off the spring I've placed above the needle, causing it to drop down and inject Grim. The fucking problem is that it works nine times out of ten. On the tenth time, it can jam. If this happens, Grim will see it, and my plan is out the window, and he'll know it was me. I'm known for poisoning my knives, my bullets, or any of my weapons. When I go after someone, I want to know they're going to die.

The needle will be dosed in Taipan venom, thanks to the newest addition to my collection. She wasn't easy to come by and cost me a pretty penny, but one drop of her venom is enough to kill one hundred men. It's painful and will only take about forty-five minutes to cause death.

My plan is to switch out Grim's magazine with my poisoned one at the Motorcycles, Mafia, and Mayhem book signing this weekend. We'll all be required to surrender our guns or knives. Grim will check his gun when he gets it back at the end of the day—his habit will be his downfall. My biggest problem will be not getting caught when I switch out the magazines. I plan to create a diversion, which should cover my tracks. Many will suspect me, but they won't be able to prove it, especially if I can get the magazine back. They'd have to have a keen eye to see the small hole I've drilled into the bottom of the magazine. Most won't even see it.

My plan is to aggravate Elora enough so she gravitates toward Grim. He has a tendency to want to protect the women he likes. Elora will be his downfall and my salvation.

Elora

Housework.

The bane of my existence.

I'm standing in the middle of my small apartment, staring at the dishes in the sink and wishing for the hundredth time I had a dishwasher. Today is Saturday, the sky outside is a brilliant blue and too nice a day to be stuck inside.

Picking up my coffee cup, I take a sip and flop onto one of my dining chairs. The dishes can wait. My cell phone rings. Turning it over, it says *Scumbag* with a pretty picture of my ex.

That's not his name, but it's what I call him now. We only dated for three months, but it was a complete waste of my time. When the call ends and goes to voicemail, I sigh in relief. The club, Defiant

Men MC, called him Toxin. One would think a name like that would have set off warning bells, but it didn't. He's not the first club boy I've dated, but he *will* be the last.

They're all the same.

Women are property.

Women are less than.

My phone rings again, but this time it's my friend, Whitney.

"Hey, girl."

"Elora," she exclaims. "What are you doing today?"

My eyes go to the dishes, but my mouth says, "Nothing. You?"

Whitney squeals into the phone, and I pull it away from my ear. "Yay, you're coming with me."

My lips turn down. I love Whitney, but she's a bit of a nerd. One time, she got me to go to a lecture on the meaning of life, and by the time it finished, I was ready to end mine or hers for making me sit through it.

"Whit, it depends on where we are going."

"An author event," she says, her voice full of excitement.

"A what?" I take another sip of my coffee.

"It's so cool. Some of my favorite authors are

going. MariaLisa deMora, Avelyn Paige, Daphne Loveling, Vera—"

"So it's a book thing?"

"Yes. All the authors and their books will be there. It's an MC, mafia, bad-boy fest. And they sometimes bring their *cover models*," Whitney shrieks.

"Whit, I don't read."

"You do."

"No, I don't."

"You do. I gave you a book by Kathleen Kelly. It was called *Savage Stalker*."

She did give me a book, and I have no idea where I put it. Reading isn't my thing, but she was so enthusiastic at the time I didn't know how to say no to her.

Shit, now I have to find it to return it.

"Can't you go alone?"

"No." All the excitement has dripped out of her tone with that one little word.

She sure is the queen of guilt-tripping. "What time?"

"Yes! I'll come get you. It's going to be fun. Wear comfortable shoes."

Whitney hangs up, and I glance at the dishes. Suddenly, they don't seem so bad. Groaning, I head into my bedroom and open my closet. I need to change, fix my hair, and apply a little makeup. Whitney is tall with long dark hair. She's one of the prettiest women I know, but she doesn't know she's pretty. Men openly stare at her, but she's oblivious, so if I'm with her, I need to look at least presentable.

I'm definitely wearing jeans, and as it's a bad-boy fest, I'll wear my black leather boots but not the six-inch heels—the two-inch heels. Whit said to wear comfortable shoes. For the top, I reach for a tight-fitting, sleeveless, black corset style and pair it with a sheer ruby-red, long-sleeved blouse. It screams available with a hint of modesty, or, as my good friend, Brandi, would say, chic biker. Better than trailer trash.

Staring in the mirror, I decide to leave my blonde hair down, but I loosely curl the ends to give me a little body. Lipsticks are my weakness. I have a plethora of them, and I know I have one in here to match the red blouse. When I find it, I paint my lips and apply some mascara.

As if on cue, there's a knock at my front door. Whit is nothing if not punctual. My small cross-body handbag is hanging on my bedroom door, and I sling it over my body and hurry to let Whit in.

"Let's go." She laughs and pulls on my hand.

"Okay, okay." I pull the door closed, and we take the elevator down to the ground floor.

"Are you going to be able to walk for hours in those?"

Laughing, I reply, "Yes, Mom."

Whitney points at her Converse. "These are more appropriate."

"Yes, if you're as tall as you are. If you're a five-foot-tall blonde standing next to an Amazonian, you need the height."

"Yes, and those... what, two inches? They make all the difference."

"Shut up."

Whitney giggles and unlocks her car. "Okay, I'll shut up." As she starts it, she gives me the biggest grin. "I'm so excited I get to meet some of my favorite authors."

"You're fangirling, and we aren't even there yet."

"Hey, how come you're not working? It's the weekend."

I'm a bartender, and it's mostly late nights and weekend work, but I arranged with my boss to have this weekend off. I've been saving for months. There are big decisions waiting for me to make up my mind about, and I decided by Sunday night I'll know which is my best course of action. Whitney is a good friend, but I haven't shared my plans with anyone. Breaking up with Toxin sort of helped put my life and where I was headed into perspective.

"Told my boss ages ago I needed this weekend off."

Whitney glances at me. "Did I screw up your plans?"

"No, no, no. Just wanted some me time."

"Aww, shit. Now I feel bad."

"Don't. You saved me from housework."

"I'm so excited." Whitney moves up and down in her seat. "It's not often I get a day to myself without the kids or Tony." Her smile is infectious. "It's going to be a cool day."

Something tells me it's going to be a *long* day.

Grim

To improve our public image, I agreed we would volunteer at the Motorcycles, Mafia, and Mayhem author signing. The event organizer, Sapphire Knight, made us all agree to a no-violence, two-day weekend. There are five MC clubs represented. As the president of the Warriors of Destruction, I decided the easiest way to ensure we wouldn't resort to beating or killing some of the other MC members was to be here myself. And looking around the venue as people are setting up, it seems the other clubs had the same idea. It's rare to see five club presidents under the same roof.

"Excuse me... uh... Mr. Grim?"

Turning around, I see a pretty little brunette with a clipboard. "It's just Grim."

"Right." She nods profusely. "I'm Jordan, one of the volunteers for the event, and as it's a friendly zone, we'll need you to surrender your weapons." Tilting my head to the side, I scowl at her, and she steps back. "All the other MCs have arrived, and they have all complied. You're the last to arrive…" Her voice goes soft, and she shifts from foot to foot.

"*All* of them gave up their weapons?"

"Y-yes?"

"And where are you storing our weapons?"

Jordan gives me a tentative smile and points toward a door where there are two solid-looking men with their arms crossed. They're dressed in security uniforms, and judging by the bulge under their jackets, they both have guns on them.

Nodding toward them, I say, "They've got guns."

"They're security."

Walking toward the two men, Jordan jogs beside me.

"You need to fill out this form." She thrusts her clipboard at me.

I take it but don't slow down. Both men see me coming and straighten up.

"I need to see the room before I let you have my gun."

They exchange a glance, and then the bigger of

the two dips his chin. He steps back, opens the door behind him, and gestures for me to look inside.

"We have five tables. Every gun, knife, brass knuckles, or any kind of fighting implement is on these tables." I move to enter the room, and he puts a hand on my chest. Locking eyes with him, he removes his hand and holds both up to placate me. "No one but me or Brett may enter this room. We are both licensed security guards, and we aim to keep everyone safe."

"So, no one but you two have been in there today?"

"Yes, sir, that's correct."

Holding out the clipboard, he takes it off me, and I pull my gun out of its holster, drop out the magazine, check she's got one at the ready, and slam the magazine back in.

"You can have it."

He nods, and I exchange my gun for the clipboard. "If you'll write down the make, the serial number, your name, and your club, we'd appreciate it."

The form takes me a moment to fill in. All the while, he holds my gun down at his side. It doesn't sit well with me not having a weapon. It's like an extension of myself, and I don't remember the last time it wasn't within easy reach.

I pass the clipboard to the other security guard, and he pulls off my form and hands it to the man holding my Glock. He holds it up, walks into the room, and puts the piece of paper down with my gun on top of it. The table has Red's pig sticker on it. Even from this distance, I'd know it anywhere.

"This is your MC's table."

I nod. "No one but you two, right?"

"Yes, sir," he replies.

"Name?"

"I'm Rex, he's Brett."

Turning to walk away, my gaze lands on Toxin. He's a sly motherfucker. He belongs to the Defiant Men MC. Toxin is only a soldier, but I don't like him or his pathetic club. The fucker crosses his arms, scowls, and gives me a chin lift. I do not return his effort to be civil. Instead, I move further into the venue. Hopefully, their president, Tank, will keep him under control. The other three MCs we have a truce with. Hell, The Soldiers of War MC are all retired war vets, and their president, Shotgun, is a friend.

Shotgun walks toward me, a grin on his big bearded face. He's only five foot nine, but there's not an ounce of fat on him. He rushes at me, and I think he's going to punch me in the gut, but he sidesteps and slaps me on the back.

"Grim," he bellows, causing all to stare. "How the fuck are you?"

I hold out my hand. "Good, Shotgun. How's life treating you?"

He takes my hand and moves in closer to me. I'm six foot seven, so I bend to hear his response.

"You ever seen so many women who are into bikers?" he whispers. "I'm getting laid tonight."

Laughing, I take a step away. He's right. None of these women are afraid of us. When I entered the room, two of them asked me which club I was with and if I could help unload their boxes of books from their car. It's nice not to be feared by regular people but an odd feeling at the same time.

Shotgun points to a table where some of his men are sitting. "We all got a table in the room. Yours is at the back. Sapphire made sure to keep us all separated. The Defiant is at the front of the room. Toxin is being his usual dickhead self."

Chuckling, I say, "Yeah, saw him on the way in. One day, I'm going to put that fucker in the ground."

Shotgun shakes his head. "But not today. Today is all about being nice and getting laid."

"I must have missed that last bit in the list of

rules Sapphire sent out."

Shotgun stops smiling and again moves closer to me and drops his voice. "That one is hard as fucking nails. Fucking hot, but her husband? I swear if looks could kill, I'd be six feet under. Don't go trying to get lucky with her. I reckon her husband would kill us in our sleep."

"Nah, he'd do it in broad daylight."

"You know him?"

"A little."

Shotgun raises his eyebrows, and his lips go into a hard line as he rocks on his heels. "Hmm… best keep away from her. So, who'd you bring with you? I'm here with my sergeant at arms, Rocky, a couple of prospects, and Byte. He's got mad computer skills. I have no fucking idea what he's doing half the time."

"Six men and me. I picked the biggest brothers to bring with me. My VP, Red, is here. You know him, yeah?"

"Yeah, he's ex-military. I'd hoped he'd join with us instead of you."

"No surprise he'd want to be in the best MC."

Shotgun bursts out laughing. "Yeah, man, you keep telling yourself that. All right, catch you later." He walks off, his eyes firmly on the ass of the woman in front of him.

"Excuse me?" Turning around, there's a female holding onto a pole and a rectangular metal bar. "Could you help me put this together?" She has a cute accent. Australian, I think.

"Sure."

"Great. Come this way." She walks to a table. "I want it here, please."

Her table has a black cloth over it. Printed on it is a logo and the name Kathleen Kelly.

"Is that you?" I ask, nodding at the name.

"Yes, I'm Kathleen, and you are?"

"Grim."

She puts down the metal bar and holds out her hand. "Pleased to meet you, Grim."

"Aussie?"

Kathleen laughs. "Yes." She picks up the metal bar. "Normally, my husband would do this, but he's off talking to MariaLisa deMora. Honestly, he's a lousy PA sometimes." She's laughing, so I know she doesn't really mean it.

"What do you need me to do?"

Kathleen hands me the metal bar, which weighs next to nothing. "This goes on the floor, and you pull it up, insert the pole at the top, and once it's fully extended, put the pole into the base. It's a banner."

"Seems easy enough."

"It is, but I'm too short."

I do as she says and erect her banner. It has her logo, name, and the words *Author of Sexy Romance* printed on it.

"I can see why you needed help. My height is definitely an advantage."

Kathleen giggles. "How tall are you?"

"Six-seven."

"Damn."

"Excuse me?" There's another woman holding a banner. "Could you help me too?"

"For a small fee, Grim would be happy to help you, Maci," Kathleen teases.

"I'll pay anything," she replies with a giggle.

"Grim, this is a fellow Aussie, Maci Dillon."

Maci thrusts her banner at me. "Nice to meet you." She's got a cute, infectious smile.

"Where do you want it?"

Maci bursts out laughing, and Kathleen goes a pretty shade of red.

Pointing, she says, "Next to my table, please."

Within the space of thirty seconds, every female author near Kathleen is asking me to erect their banners. Some openly flirt, others just thank me profusely.

I'm on to my fifth banner when Red appears at my side. "Need any help?"

"It seems all the authors are short and need help putting these up."

"Want me to take over?"

"Yes. Ran into Shotgun, said we had a table at the back of the room."

"Yeah, keep going, Prez, and you'll find it." Red is only an inch or two shorter than me and leans in, whispering, "The women at this thing are mighty friendly. I'm getting laid tonight."

It seems Shotgun and Red have the same one-track mind. Laughing, I slap him on the shoulder and leave him to do the banners.

My men are all at the back of the room. Boxer is sitting at the table, his arms folded, looking anything but friendly. When he sees me, he straightens up, but the scowl on his face remains the same. The others are chatting with authors or helping erect their banners or boxes of books.

"Boxer," I say by way of a greeting.

"Prez."

"What's got you looking so happy?"

He stands and moves around the table. "Why am I here?"

Boxer is six feet of muscle, has a shaved head, is

covered in intricate tattoos, and when he smiles, which is rare, he has a gold tooth. He's one of my best soldiers—always follows orders and always has my back. My sergeant at arms, Torch, gets frustrated with him. He's supposed to have my back, but Boxer is never far from me in a fight. What Torch doesn't know is I saved Boxer's life years ago, and he feels indebted to me. Obviously not enough to want to be at an author signing.

"The Defiant is here. Torch had a family thing on today, so I chose you to make sure no one stabs me in the back."

Boxer's chest puffs out, the scowl disappears, and he does a quick glance around the room. "Didn't see them. Anyone in particular I should be on the lookout for?"

"Toxin is here."

"Fucking little sneaky cunt." He moves in closer and whispers, "I could kill the motherfucker if you'd like?"

"It's all good, Boxer. And we promised no violence, remember?"

"I'd make it quick, so minimal violence."

Chuckling, I shake my head. "No."

He grunts and leans against the table. "Fine." Boxer gestures toward Rocket with a slight dip of his head. "Rocket has a message for you from the organizer."

"Sapphire?"

"Fuck if I know what her name is. She's got pretty hair."

"She's married."

"I didn't say I wanted to fuck her. I just like her hair."

Rocket sees me staring at him and says something to the woman he's talking to. She laughs, then he walks over to me.

"Hey, Prez, did you just get here?"

Shaking my head, I say, "No, I've been helping them put up their banners and shit."

Rocket laughs. "Yeah, I've done a few of those myself. Sapphire asked me to ask you if we'd participate in a group photo with the authors. She'd like all of the MC lined up on the staircase with the authors on the steps below."

"So long as we aren't next to the Defiant, I'm cool with that."

"Cool. We have to be there at..." he glances at his watch, "... in twenty minutes."

"Fine."

"Do you need me for anything, Grim?" His eyes are on the ass of the woman he was talking to. She's bent over, pulling books out of a box.

"No." He turns to leave. "But Rocket?" He stops. "Best behavior, yeah?"

"Always." Rocket winks at me and goes back to the woman.

Shifting my focus to Boxer, I ask, "Why aren't you helping?"

"No one's asked me to."

Putting a hand on his shoulder, I say, "Boxer, we are here to improve our public image. To make nice with the locals so maybe the law will cut us some slack. Try smiling and being friendly. Hell, you might get lucky."

"I've got a woman. I don't need any more." He scowls as he peers past me. "Five-O just walked in."

Making a beeline for us is Marshal Johnny Saint-Mark. He's had a hard-on for us since he moved here six months ago.

"Well, well, well, if it isn't my favorite MC, the Warriors of Destruction."

"Aww shucks, Marshal, I didn't know you liked us that much."

The man smiles at me. He's Latino and has perfectly straight white teeth. He reminds me of a wolverine. Deadly.

He laughs. "I don't." The marshal tips his hat.

"This is your friendly reminder to play nice today."

"Or what?"

"Or I'll put you in the ground myself."

Laughing, I nod. "I'd love to see you try."

His perfect smile disappears, and he takes a step toward me. Boxer, perceiving a threat, moves closer to my side.

"Don't think I won't do what I need to do to keep innocent people from getting hurt."

Holding up my hands, I say, "We've called a truce. You'll get no trouble from my MC. The Defiant Men are the ones you should be harassing. Not us."

He sneers at me and moves along.

"Why does that fucker insist on giving you such a hard time?" Boxer watches the marshal as he threads his way through the crowd.

"He's only doing his job."

"Nah, it's more than that. If he sees you out in public, he makes a point of trying to bust your balls. Did you fuck his momma or something?"

Laughing, I shake my head. "No. He's overcompensating for his lack of height, and we used to be friends."

Boxer chuckles. "Little man syndrome? He's probably got a small dick too."

"I wouldn't know. I haven't checked."

A squealing noise erupts over the speaker system. "Good morning, everyone. We are thirty minutes away from showtime. Can all the authors and MCs please make your way over to the staircase so we can get a group photo? Thank you." Another squeal happens and then silence.

"How's my hair?" Boxer asks.

Rolling my eyes at his bald head, I say, "Perfect."

With me in front of my men, we work our way through the crowd to the staircase. The Defiant Men are on one side, and we're on the other. Their president stares at me with no expression, and I ignore him. Like Toxin, his soldier, I have no use for him. His name is Tank, and not because he's fit. The fucker is a slob, and I'm surprised a motorcycle can hold his weight.

"Grim?"

It's the cute Aussie author, Maci.

"Yeah?"

"Would you mind if I stood in front of you?"

"Hell, honey, you can stand next to me if you'd like."

She giggles nervously but stands next to me. "Thank you." Her smile gets bigger as she stands side-on, boobs out, looking forward.

Red winks at me and raises his eyebrows. He's

not known for being subtle and clearly thinks I'm in with a chance with the cute blonde.

Sapphire is at the bottom of the stairs and claps her hands together loudly. "Okay, everyone. Tallest to shortest on the stairs. We've got ten minutes before the VIPs are allowed in, so places."

Amazingly, everyone does as they are told and climb the stairs, taking their positions.

"How the hell did you get to stand there?" Kathleen asks Maci.

She sticks out her tongue. "I asked."

"Hussy."

"You wish."

The two women burst out laughing, and Kathleen stands in front of Maci.

"You could stand on the other side of me?"

Kathleen smiles at me. "My husband is watching. And I kind of molested Wander Agular at the last signing I went to. I don't think he'd appreciate me doing the same to you."

"You touched Wander?" Maci asks.

"I was only touching his T-shirt... which was attached to his chest."

"And you called *me* a hussy?"

Kathleen laughs and goes a shade of red. "I really love my squishy husband," she says to me as she points to a man with dark hair smiling at her from across the room. "He belongs to me." She waves at him, and he waves back.

Maci leans down and touches her shoulder. "You are so lucky."

Kathleen nods. "Yeah, I am."

From the tone of her voice, I can tell she's in love with her husband.

"How long have you two been married?"

"Twenty-three years this year, but I've known him since I was sixteen. We were friends for a long time. Still are."

"Okay, everyone, look at me," the photographer yells to get everyone's attention. "Smile."

Someone yells out, "Spaghetti."

The authors all yell spaghetti as the photographer clicks away on his camera.

"Okay, silly photo time. Pull a face in three... two... one."

I simply smile at him while the women around me pull faces or laugh at one another. He nods to Sapphire, who moves from her place on the stairs.

"Thank you all for coming. Doors are open soon. If you need anything, ask one of the volunteers. Have fun and sell loads of books." Sapphire throws her hair over one shoulder and strides away from us.

Maci touches my bicep. "Thank you."

"She'll buy you a drink later," Kathleen says.

"There's a bar?"

Kathleen laughs. "How come I know there's a bar and you don't?"

"You drink more than me?"

"Hardly."

The two women walk away from us, engrossed in their conversation.

"You right, Prez?" Red asks.

"Yeah. These women are a different breed, yeah?"

Red's smile becomes bigger. "Friendly, I like them."

"Keep it in your pants."

He barks out a laugh. "Not if I don't have to." Red goes down the stairs and puts his arm around the woman I saw him talking to earlier. She laughs as he whispers something in her ear, then he shoots me a wink.

"Red's getting laid," Boxer states.

"The man is a horn dog," Wheels says as we all watch Red walk away.

"Yeah, he is," I agree.

A sneer crosses Goat's features as he glares at

the Defiant Men MC. He takes a step in their direction. Reaching out, I place a hand on his shoulder.

"Not here, not today, brother."

Goat stops, his top lip curling up in disgust. "I don't trust them, and I don't enjoy being in the same room as them, Prez."

"I'll second that," Link replies.

"We promised to play nice," I say in a strong not-to-be-fucked-with voice.

Goat squints up at me. "Do they know that?"

I cock my head to the side. "Come on, let's go to our spot at the back of the room away from them. You are all your brother's keepers today. No violence." I fix my eyes on Boxer. "Which means no, you can't kill them quickly."

Link punches Boxer in the arm and laughs. "You said that, didn't you?"

"What if I did?" Boxer walks ahead of him, and the crowd of females parts for him as if on some level they can sense how dangerous he can be.

Goat walks with me through the crowd.

Shotgun appears at my side. "You okay, Grim?"

"Yeah."

"Couldn't help but notice the tension between you and the Defiant."

"Bunch of cocksuckers," Goat says.

"Yeah, but we don't have the troubles with them you have."

"No, you don't," I agree.

"Maybe it's time you let things go?"

I give Shotgun a sideways glance and say, "I appreciate the advice, but you didn't lose a patched-in member to them, and we did."

"I remember. But if my memory serves me, you couldn't prove it."

"It was them." Goat glares at Shotgun.

Shotgun holds up his hands. "I believe you."

The longer this conversation goes on, the more I can see Goat losing his shit and doing something we're all going to regret.

Staring at Goat, I say, "Like you, we promised a violence-free weekend. We're men of our word. It won't be us who breaks the truce."

Goat sucks in a breath, and his nostrils flare as he walks ahead of me to our table.

"Is he going to let sleeping dogs lie?"

"Don't test him, man. I respect you, but this is my MC. You worry about your men, and I'll worry about mine."

Shotgun puffs out his cheeks. "Sorry, man, I didn't mean any offense."

Nodding, I continue walking through the crowd to my men at the back of the room. Goat is sitting in a chair, scowling at the floor. Link is staring down at him with a concerned expression on his face.

Red appears next to me. "Did I miss something?"

"No."

Before I can say more, a male voice comes over the loudspeaker. "Welcome to the third Motorcycles, Mafia, and Mayhem Author Signing Event. As a reminder, all models and members of the MCs are not to be touched unless they invite you to. I repeat, don't touch the models or members of the MCs. Have fun, and remember, your authors are excited to see you as much as you are them, but they can be shy creatures, so make sure you say hello to them." Another loud squeal sounds and then silence.

Red's author says, "Here they come." She's smiling and is clearly excited from the way she's bobbing up and down on the balls of her feet.

To Red, I say, "Don't touch the MC unless we invite them to?"

Link laughs. "They can touch me all they want."

A woman rushing past bursts out laughing. "You might regret that."

I move behind the table and address my men.

"Okay, on your best behavior. Keep away from the Defiant. Have fun and *be friendly*." My gaze lands on Boxer, who rolls his eyes and tries to smile.

The marshal walks past our table, tipping his hat at us, and I give him a chin lift. A smile warms his face, but it quickly disappears. Boxer is right—he has a hard-on for me, and I have no idea why.

Elora

The doors to the event open, and Whitney moves to the front of the crowd, pulling me with her. We enter the room, and she's got her head down, staring at a map as she sidesteps people to get through the venue.

"Whit, where are we going?"

"I want to see Manda Mellett before her line gets too long."

"I'm assuming that's an author?"

Whit rolls her eyes. "Yes."

A hand on my arm stops me in my tracks. Turning, Toxin's light green eyes meet mine.

"Not today," I say with a groan.

"Aww, don't be like that, Elora. I'm so glad you're here."

"I didn't know *you* were here."

"Yes, you did," Whitney states. I shake my head at her. "I told you real MC would be here. It's why I wanted you to come."

Sighing, I roll my eyes. "I didn't know *you'd* be here." Twisting my arm out of his grasp, I move away from him. "We're done, over, never to be repeated *ever* again."

"Don't say that. I've missed you."

Closing my eyes, I take a deep breath and exhale slowly. I plaster a smile on my lips and open my eyes. "I don't care. You cheated on me. You mistreated me, and I deserve so much better. I can't believe I stayed with you as long as I did. You're toxic, Toxin, and we are over."

Grabbing Whitney's hand, I march through the crowd but not before I hear, "I'll be seeing you, Elora."

Holding up my hand, I give him the bird, but I don't stop dragging Whitney through the crowd until she stops me.

"What?" I say impatiently.

"This is Manda Mellett."

Standing in front of us is a short red-headed woman with a big smile. "You're a fan?"

"I have read *all* of your books." Whitney gushes.

"My favorite is *StoryTeller's Tale*."

"Thank you," Manda replies.

Whitney picks up a book off her table. "Could I buy this one, please? I don't have it in paperback yet, only on my Kindle."

"Of course."

Moving away from them a little, I walk further into the room. There's table after table of authors with their books piled high. Some readers burst into tears as they meet the authors, who either look confused, uncomfortable, or amused.

Whit waves at me, and I point toward the back of the room. She nods, and I keep moving. The further away from Toxin I get, the happier I'll be. My cell phone sounds, and I pull it out of my bag. It's an unknown number. I don't answer the call but hit decline and throw it back in. It's sort of a rule not to answer my phone if I don't know the person. I'm thinking it's probably Toxin, and I have no desire to talk to him ever again.

Glancing over my shoulder, I see Whitney is still talking to Manda, so I keep walking straight into a brick wall. Well, a brick wall in the shape of a man.

"Sorry."

"Lady, why don't you watch where you're walking?" He's sort of smiling at me, a gold tooth peeking between his lips.

"I'm so sorry. I was trying to keep an eye on my friend, but I should have been looking where I was going."

"Yep, watching where I walk has always worked well for me."

Now he's pissing me off. "Really?" I put my hands on my hips. "I said I was sorry. Why don't you cut me some slack?"

His eyebrows go up in surprise. "What did you say?"

A hand lands on his shoulder. "Boxer, is there a problem here?"

The hand belongs to a six-foot-seven man, and from the patches on his cut, he's the president of the Warriors of Destruction.

"No, no, no. There's no problem here. I apologized, and now I'm going on my merry way."

He smiles down at me, then asks his man, "We good?"

"Yes, Prez."

"See, I told you. We're good." I'm nodding like an idiot.

He holds out his hand. "I'm Grim."

"I'm sworn off bikers."

"That's your name?" Grim grins at me, and I feel

a blush creep up my neck.

"Elora." I take his hand in mine, and a tingle works its way from my palm to my chest. "Oh." I quickly drop his hand.

"Nice to meet you, Elora."

Grim sort of drawls out my name, and I like the way he says it. Smiling up at him, I continue my path to the back of the room. There are chairs along a wall, and I sit my butt down, waiting for Whitney. My phone sounds again, and I pull it out of my bag. It's work. With a groan, I open the text message.

Work: *Hey, Elora! We need you to start a little earlier on Monday. Inventory is at noon okay?*

It's my first weekend off in over six months. Being a bartender, I usually work every weekend and all the night shifts I can get, but lately, it's all become a drag. My boss, Bobby, is a good guy, but he pays minimum wage, and I survive on tips, just like everyone else in my profession.

Taking a deep breath, I let it out slowly and raise my gaze to the crowd before me. Not three feet from me is the behemoth, Grim. He cocks his head to the side and sits next to me.

"You okay?"

"Work," I say as I hold up my phone.

"You have to go in?"

"They want me to start early on Monday."

"Today is Saturday."

I frown. "I know. It's just I wanted the weekend to think. Now, I either have to tell him if I'm coming in early or if I'm not coming in at all."

"Where do you work?"

"Bobby's Bar over in Chinatown."

"Aah, Defiant's territory."

"Yeah, there's another reason to leave. Fucking bikers."

Grim raises his eyebrows and sits back. "Right." He stands and moves to his brethren.

Great.

Twice in the space of ten minutes, I've angered a soldier and now the president of the Warriors of Destruction. Grim glances over his shoulder at me and exchanges words with Boxer, who scowls at me, then Grim shrugs. Both men chat before Grim walks off into the crowd without a backward glance. Not wanting to have another confrontation, I reread Bobby's message on my phone.

In the past six months, I've saved like a demon so I could comfortably leave my job, find another, move or maybe all three. But staring at the message, maybe I'm better to play it safe? At least I have a job, and my apartment isn't so bad. My phone beeps, and it's a text message from an unknown number.

> **Unknown number:** *Come on, beautiful. You have to forgive me. You're my girl, right? Love T*

I groan.

> **Me:** *Not a girl. I'm a woman and I was never yours.*

Then I block that number too. *Seriously, what does he need to get the hint?* Toxin was a mistake. Three months of misery. Well, not all three months. The first month, we dated and flirted at the bar where I worked, then I got invited to a club party, and we hung out more, and for about six weeks, I thought we were a couple. But, apparently, for a guy like Toxin, spell it out.

When did dating get to be so goddamn hard?

In all honesty, I thought he'd be glad to get rid of me. Toxin didn't seem to want a monogamous relationship, and I don't know how to do it any other way. A shadow falls across me, and I look up.

"Girl, where have you been?" Whitney's infectious grin beams down at me.

"Waiting for you." She's carrying two bags of books. "How many books have you bought?"

Whitney shrugs. "It's my vice, like crack or cocaine."

"Babe, they are the same thing."

"You sure?"

Chuckling, I stand and take a bag off her. "Yep, pretty sure."

Whitney shrugs. "Come on, there are more books to buy."

Tucking my phone into my bag, I say, "So, where to?"

Whitney reaches out and touches my arm. "You okay?"

Today I must be wearing my heart on my sleeve if a complete stranger and now Whitney can read me so easily.

"Work stuff."

"We can talk and walk?"

"Nah, let's not." A crease forms between her eyebrows. "Honestly, it's no big deal."

"It's a big enough deal that you're frowning."

"Maybe later. Right now, I want to know who

you're excited to see and why."

Whitney does a little jump and nods. "Okay, down this way are some of the Aussie authors. Honestly, I could listen to them talk all day. Some authors are shy, but they aren't."

"Wait. Are some of these women shy? Then why the hell do they put themselves out there?"

Whitney tilts her head to the side and looks me dead in the eyes. "For the readers. They write these incredible stories and then release them into the world for us." She stops and looks around the room. "Book people are the best people."

"You mean they write porn, and you get off on it?"

Shaking her head, she says, "Romance, not porn." Then she smiles. "But some of them are hot." Whitney fans herself as she walks toward another table.

Laughing at her, I follow.

Grim

Elora is smiling at her friend as she joins the crowd of women. She can't be over five feet tall, while her friend is a good foot taller than her. Elora is blonde with hazel eyes and is wearing a see-through red blouse with a black corset under it. Her whole demeanor screams biker chick, but she's made it clear she doesn't date bikers.

"Penny for your thoughts?" Red asks as he follows my gaze.

"I don't like being without my gun."

Red chuckles. "Last I checked..." he points at Elora, "... that's not a gun."

"She's cute, sassy, and doesn't date bikers."

"Aah, a challenge for you, then?"

Ignoring his comment, I say, "Do a sweep of the

room. Make sure no one can get to our weapons."

"And the woman?"

"Keep your eyes and hands off her."

Red laughs, shoves me, and moves into the crowd. It amazes me no one gets out of his way. They smile and flirt with him, but not one of them appears scared. It's strange.

With a quick sweep of the room, I easily find Elora and her red shirt, although it's easier to spot her friend—she must be one of the tallest women in here. Elora is shifting from foot to foot while her friend chats with one of the Aussie authors. It's clear she isn't part of this crowd.

"Uh... excuse me?"

To my left is a woman. She's maybe forty, a little overweight, pushing a small cart.

"Yes?"

"You're one of the bikers, aren't you?"

"Yes, ma'am." I hold out my hand. "My name's Grim, and I'm president of the Warriors of Destruction MC."

She swaps her wallet to her other hand and shakes my hand. "I'm Rita Turnbull. I live here in Lake Conroe."

"Nice to meet you."

"Could I ask you a question?"

"Sure." I point at the chairs where Elora was sitting. "Did you want to take a load off?"

Rita's face goes beet red, and she nods emphatically as she pushes her cart toward the chairs. "Yes, please. I love these things, but it doesn't feel like the air-conditioning is working very well."

She's right, the room does feel a little warm. Rita flops onto a chair, and I take a seat, leaving a chair between us.

"So, what did you want to ask me?"

Her face goes a deeper shade of red. "How did you become a biker?" Surprised at her question, I'm a little lost for words. "I don't mean to be rude. It's just I read all these books, and I've never met a real biker before, let alone a president of an MC."

"My dad was the president of the Warriors of Destruction. I guess it was the family business. My brother, Todd... we called him Hammer... was in too. He passed a while back."

"Gang war?"

"No." I shake my head. "He got pancreatic cancer."

Rita's face softens, and her eyes drop to the floor. She reaches over and touches my hand. "I'm so sorry for your loss and my invasive questions. I didn't mean to be so... so..."

"Nosy?" Rita pulls her hand away. "It's okay. It was nearly five years ago when Hammer died. My dad died in a drive-by. They never caught who did it."

Rita looks me in the eyes. "I'm so sorry. How long ago was it?"

"He died three years before my brother, so eight."

"So much loss."

Tilting my head to the side, I give her a half smile. "Yes, but they both lived life to the fullest, and losing those you love gives you a reason to live each day like it's your last. I'm forever grateful to my father and my brother. They were good men who were taken too soon. And I got to follow in my father's footsteps. I think he'd be proud."

Boxer comes to stand near me, arms folded, sunglasses on, staring straight ahead. I follow his gaze, and it lands on Toxin. He's got Elora by the arm, and from the expression on her face, she isn't happy to see him.

"Excuse me," I say to Rita without taking my eyes off Elora.

Striding across the room, I put myself between Elora and Toxin.

"Fuck off, Grim. This ain't got nothing to do with you." Toxin bounces on the balls of his feet, looking around me to see Elora.

"The lady doesn't seem to like you."

"How the fuck would you know what she likes?"

Moving closer to him, Toxin is forced to move back. I'm a good four inches taller than him, and I use my height to tower over him.

"Elora doesn't want you touching her."

"Elora doesn't... how the fuck do you know her name?"

"Enough." Elora sidesteps Boxer and stands in front of both of us. She pokes Toxin in the chest. "You need to leave me alone." Then she throws a hand in the air. "And *you* need to mind your own business."

Turning on her heel, she walks away, shaking her head and talking to herself. When I shift my attention to Toxin, he's not watching her, he's watching me.

"You got something to say?"

His face twists into a scowl. "Not fucking likely." Toxin starts to leave, then stops. "You know she's a club girl, yeah? Works in our territory, lives in our territory. I mean, if you're after sloppy—"

"Finish that sentence and I'll make sure you eat

45

through a straw for the rest of your life."

A grin spreads across his face, and he raises his eyebrows and shakes a finger at me. "I'll be seeing you, Grim."

Toxin strides through the crowd. Whatever they see on his face, the women make a path for him. Boxer stands next to me.

"Can I kill him now?"

"No, you can't. You all promised to behave."

We both turn our heads to see Sapphire Knight standing there with her hands on her hips, glaring at us.

"He was kidding."

"No, I wasn't."

With a sigh, I place my hand on Boxer's shoulder. "He *was* kidding." I tighten my grip on his shoulder to hammer home my point.

"Good." Sapphire smiles at the small crowd that has gathered. "Nothing to see here, folks. Make sure you come by my table to get a free e-book." To me, she whispers, "Behave."

"Yes, ma'am."

Boxer, with his shades still on, nods once. Sapphire moves away from us.

When I'm certain she's not within hearing distance, I say, "Take Goat, get a fix on Toxin and the woman. I want to make sure she's safe."

"Why?"

"Because he's fucking bad news, that's why."

"No, not him, the woman?" Boxer pulls off his shades, his expression perplexed.

"Because I said so."

His lips turn down at the sides, but he moves off, and I know he'll do as he's told. Scrubbing a hand over my face, I look back to where Rita was sitting. She's gone, and I wonder what she thinks of me and the other MC members now.

Elora

Fucking Toxin won't leave me alone, and now Grim seems to think I need saving. I've escaped to the relative safety of the ladies' room to escape the male testosterone floating around out there. Not that there should be a male-dominated space as the room is ninety-five percent female.

Walking out of the cubicle, I walk into an older woman. "My apologies."

"Are you okay?"

"Sorry?"

"I was talking to Grim when he came to your rescue. It looked pretty heated."

"You're a friend of Grim's?"

"Oh, no. I'm Rita. I was only asking him some questions. Sapphire said we should try to get to know the bikers, and nothing was off-limits. He's a lovely man."

"I'm sure he is, but I didn't need rescuing."

"That other one looked mean."

"Toxin? He's normally harmless, if not a little thick. The man isn't taking the hint."

"Oh, I so get that." Rita laughs and slaps my arm. "Back in the day, I beat them off with a stick."

"Rita, you don't look old. I bet you still do."

She laughs harder, and her face goes red. Rita holds up a hand with a wedding band on it. "I've been caught. Ronnie is a good man. We're happy."

"Well, I should get back."

"Uh-huh. Such a pity about Grim's family." Rita turns away from me.

"What happened to his family?"

As though we are conspirators, Rita moves in closer and lowers her voice. "Well, some eight years ago, his father, who was president of the Warriors of Destruction, was killed in a drive-by, and then five years ago, his brother, Hammer, died of pancreatic cancer. Of course, Grim followed in his father's footsteps and took up the mantle."

"I thought you and Grim weren't friends?"

Rita winks at me. "We're not. I think he needed someone to talk to and... well, I was there."

Sensing Rita likes the drama, I smile and step away. "That was very nice of you."

"Only doing what any good God-fearing woman would do. You know, most of the MC has been very nice."

"You've talked to a lot of them?"

"Oh yes. It's my favorite genre to read."

Turning on the tap, I wash my hands. "Well, it was nice talking to you."

"You too, honey."

Smiling at her, I hurry out of the bathroom and search for Whitney. She's talking to Grim.

Fantastic.

Walking up to the two of them, I smile at her. "So where to?"

"Elora, have you met Grim?"

Jesus, could this day get any worse?

"Yes."

Whitney glances from Grim to me, a crease forming between her brows. "Okay. Uh…"

"Toxin is bad news," Grim states.

"Yep, I know."

"So are the Defiant Men."

"Yep, know that too."

Grim folds his arms across his chest, the fabric of his T-shirt straining. "If you know that, why are you their club girl?"

My mouth drops open, and I make a high-pitched squealing noise. "A-a what?"

Grim's arms drop to his sides, and from his expression, he realizes I'm no such thing.

"Did you just call me a club girl? For the Defiant Men, no less?"

"Toxin said—"

"Toxin is a no-good lying sack of shit who I stupidly dated for three months. Hell, it wasn't even really that long. Well, it was for me, but not or him." I throw my arms up in the air. "None of it matters. I. Am. Not. A. Club. *Girl.*"

Grim smirks and then quickly covers his mouth with a hand to hide his amusement. "I can see that. I apologize."

"Are you laughing at me?"

"Elora—"

Holding up a hand to silence Whitney, I say, "No, Whit. He's laughing at *me.*"

"I'm really not. It's just you're, what, five foot, and I'm six foot seven. It's kind of hard to be intimidated by someone who's—"

"Short?" I say with ice in my voice.

"I was going to say short, but I think feisty is probably the better adjective."

51

My hands go to my hips, and I cock out a hip and point at him. "*You* don't know me."

"No, I don't, but maybe I want to."

His admission causes me to freeze, and I'm lost for words. Whitney barks out a giggle, and it's enough to kick-start my brain again.

"Biker. I don't do bikers."

Turning, I walk into the crowd. I can hear Whitney calling to me as I duck and weave through the crowd. I'm almost at the front door when she catches up with me.

"Elora, please don't go." The tone of her voice makes me stop. "Please?"

Rolling my eyes toward the heavens, and all I see is the ceiling. That right there is what my life has been like—shooting for the stars and tripping over a rock—dating a good-looking, funny biker—Toxin—who used me and threw me away.

But none of this is Whitney's fault. She's always been a friend to me. Sighing, I turn around.

"Sorry."

Whitney grabs my hand. "If you really want to go, we can."

See what I mean? She's the best. Even though this is her thing, Whitney is willing to leave to keep me happy. *Why can't men be like this?*

"Could we maybe put the books in the car, take a breather, and start again?"

A huge smile creeps across her face. "Yes." Whitney jumps up in the air.

"Where are your books?"

Her hands are empty.

"I left them with Grim."

Whitney turns and moves to the side. Walking toward us is Grim. It's interesting watching the women smile at him as he powers through the crowd. He pays them no attention, his eyes on me. A small smile plays on his lips, and when he reaches us, he holds out the bags to Whitney.

"Thought you might need these."

Whitney takes them, but he doesn't break eye contact with me. Grim stops, tilts his head, gives me a two-fingered wave, then turns around and walks back the way he came.

"Oh my God, that was hot," Whitney murmurs.

The man has a nice ass as he strides through the room. There's an air of confidence about him, and it's as if everyone in the room can sense it as he walks by. The women smile at him and move out of the way, and the few men in the room give him a chin lift as he walks past. Grim certainly has a way about him.

"He's okay."

Whitney bursts out laughing. "I'd give anything to have a man look at me the way he just did you."

"I thought you and Tony were happy?"

Whitney shrugs. "We are."

"Man trouble?"

"Ladies, how are you both?"

Toxin is standing behind us, a wolfish grin on his face.

"Fuck off," I blurt out and head for the door.

"What she said," Whitney replies as she hurries to catch up with me.

When she's matching me step for step, I say, "He's such a douche."

"Seems like I'm not the only one with man trouble."

"Come on, I'll buy you a Coke, and you can tell me all about it."

"Coke Zero, please."

"You still on a health kick?"

"If I were, I'd be drinking water, not poison in a can."

Laughing, we hold out our wrists to be stamped so we can get back in and walk to the vending machine outside.

"You get the drinks, and I'll put the books in

the car."

Nodding, I dig through my small bag, searching for change.

"What do you need?"

Groaning, I glare up at Toxin. "Nothing from you."

"Aww, don't be like that, babe."

"Don't call me babe."

He puts his hands in his pockets and rocks on his heels. "I'm trying here."

"Toxin, it's too late. You're trying because you got caught, and now you're trying to fix it out of guilt. Just leave me alone."

"Guilt? I didn't know we were exclusive. We never talked about it." Toxin's lips are screwed up and to the side.

"Yeah, see, that's the difference between us. I was in it, you weren't."

Toxin leans against the vending machine. "Come on, we never said we were exclusive."

"So, if I'd slept with one of your friends, you would have been okay with it?"

Toxin tilts his head to the side. "I see your point."

He appears genuinely conflicted. Toxin sighs and runs a hand through his hair. I'm almost convinced he's sorry.

"We had fun, though, didn't we?"

"We did."

"You know, she was only a onetime thing. Sara's a club girl. All the guys have done her."

And that's when I knew he wasn't sorry at all. Justifying his indiscretion by saying all the guys had done her speaks volumes. Toxin is six three, with light green eyes, tanned, and muscular. He's a good-looking guy and smooth with the ladies. You'd think being a bartender, my radar would have gone off, but he played the long game and got to know me. Played it cool.

I'm an idiot.

Whitney appears beside me. "Is everything okay?"

"Yep. Toxin was just leaving." I smile at him.

Toxin sucks in a breath between gritted teeth and wanders away.

"What did you ever see in him?"

"He's pretty."

Whitney's lips turn down. "Pretty awful. He's one of those people who looks good on the outside, but the longer you get to know them, the uglier they get. Remember that girl we knew, Lita?"

"Oh yeah, dark brown hair, green eyes, big tits."

"Yeah, she was a pretty package, but the longer I

spent with her, the uglier she got. Now, whenever I see her, I can't understand what men or even her girlfriends see in her. She's awful."

"You're saying Toxin is like her?"

"Yeah, and Toxin? Seriously, what kind of name is that?"

"Club name."

"Real name?"

"Rupert."

"Really?"

Laughing, I shake my head. "No idea. I never asked."

Whitney laughs. "Right. Although he does look like a Rupert."

"Coke Zero?"

"Yeah." Whitney leans up against the vending machine. "Do you have enough change?"

Frowning, I dig in my bag. "Uh... I think so?" Whitney reaches into her bag and puts coins into the machine. "Sorry."

"Dude, no biggie."

"You want a Coke?"

"Yeah."

The cans fall out of the machine, and Whitney picks them up. "Shall we sit and talk for a bit?"

"I'd like that. There are some seats over there in

the shade." I point to an area a little away from us.

"Good spotting." Whitney hustles over to the chairs and pulls out her map for the author signing. "I only need to see a couple more."

Feeling bad she's cutting her day short, I say, "You've barely done one aisle. If I avoid all the men in the building, it'll be fine."

Whitney smirks. "Have you seen some of the models? Surely, you don't want to avoid them too?"

"Models?"

"Yeah, the cover models for the books. A lot of the authors have them sitting at their tables with them. Most are really sweet." She peers down at her drink. "You sure you don't mind?"

"Yeah. I think Toxin finally has the hint. Speaking of men, are you and Tony okay?"

Whitney nods. "Yes. He doesn't get why I like to go to these things." She lifts her gaze to me. "Books are my escape. I know it's all fiction and not real life, but sometimes I want Tony to... see me." She sighs. "After twelve years of marriage and three kids, I guess it's pretty stupid."

"No, it's not. You were a girlfriend and wife first. It's normal for you to want him to still think you're the hottest thing on the planet. But, girl, when was the last time you showed him you were?"

"What do you mean?"

"When was the last time you dressed up and..." I shake my chest, "... showed him what God gave you?"

Whitney's face reddens. "It's been a while. It's hard, you know? I'm chauffeuring kids around, keeping a clean house, working, and sometimes I just want to sleep." I laugh. "Take today. I had to ask my mom to look after the kids as Tony is playing golf. It never occurs to him to ask if it's okay if he plays golf every Saturday, but me? I've gotta do it all."

"Tell him. Men are stupid."

"I shouldn't have to tell him."

"Honey, Tony loves you. But sometimes they take things for granted."

Whitney chews on her bottom lip and opens her can of soda. "Maybe I take him for granted too." She takes a sip. "But I didn't get hitched to him to take the place of his mother. I need more."

Laughing, I say, "Women want a man like their father because they see how their father treats their mother and want that same relationship. Men want a woman like their mother so they can be mothered."

Whitney shakes her head. "I'm screwed."

Reaching out, I put my hand over hers. "No, you're not. You're nothing like Tony's mother." I chuckle. "I've said it before, and I'll say it again... men are stupid. Spell it out for him, but do it in a nice I'm-not-attacking-you way."

Whitney nods. "I can try."

"Come on, let's go back in and see all your favorite authors."

Grim

There are hundreds of women here and only a handful of men. I've been felt up by more women than I have in my entire life, and from the way all of my men are standing behind our table, I'm thinking they must have had their fair share of unwanted attention too. All except for Red—he's loving it. The man is carrying boxes, books—hell, anything a pretty young thing wants him to.

"Prez?"

"Yeah, Boxer?"

"I'm about done."

"It's not even lunchtime."

He unfolds his arms and slips his hands into his pockets. "There are too many people."

Reaching out, I touch his arm lightly. "Why don't

you take a break? Go outside and escape the madness for a while?"

Boxer nods once and makes a beeline for the doors without a backward glance.

"Fifty dollars says he doesn't come back," Goat jokes.

"He'll be back," Wheels states as he gestures to Boxer's retreating form. "He won't leave Grim alone for long. Boxer is loyal."

"And I'm not?" Goat asks.

"Fuck off. You know that's not what I meant. The man owes Grim, and he won't rest until the debt is repaid. He just doesn't cope well with crowds, is all."

"Excuse me?" Standing in front of us is a short older woman.

"Yes?" I say.

"Could I get a photo with you all?"

"I'll take it," Red says, appearing out of nowhere.

The woman smiles brightly at him and hands over her cell phone. "Take as many as you like." She bustles in behind the table and puts her arm around my waist. "I'm Wendy."

"Grim."

"Oh, I know." Wendy looks to her right. "Move in,

fellas, and don't forget to smile." Red takes a photograph, and she shakes her head. "Honey, could you hold the camera up a little or stand on a chair?"

"Sure." Red grabs a chair and takes a few pictures, then holds out her cell phone to her.

Wendy flicks through the images, her smile growing. "Thank you." She holds a hand to her chest. "If you take the photos from up high, I don't have a double chin."

Goat laughs. "I had a girlfriend who used to do that, and I always wondered why."

Wendy wrinkles her nose at him and giggles. "Now you know. Thank you all."

Wendy blends into the crowd.

"It's going to be a long day." Link moves to stand next to me.

He's the same height as me but is a little leaner with shorter hair and a lot more tattoos. Most of mine, except for one, are black and gray while Link likes tattoos of color. The front of his neck has a dagger with red roses on either side. On the hilt of the dagger are the words 'love' and 'loyalty.'

"You ready to leave too?"

Link rubs his hands together and gives me a wolfish grin. "Nope. Too much pussy in this room.

I'm beginning to think Red had this right. I'm going to get laid." He rocks on his heels. "Hey, where's the cute short blonde you were talking to earlier?"

"Off-limits."

"Aww… come on, Prez. She's cute." Raising an eyebrow, I face him. Link takes a step away. "Off-limits, yep, she's off-limits."

Nodding once, I survey the crowd for her. Elora is certainly a whole lot of confusion in one small package. I'm not even sure I *am* interested. Link is right, she is cute, but she also said she's sworn off bikers, and she lives and works in Defiant Men territory. *If* I wanted to see her, it would be a problem.

"So, you like her?"

My lips turn down. "I didn't say that."

Link cocks his head to the side. "What are you saying?"

"Elora is sworn off bikers."

"Elora?" Link says with a grin.

"She dated Toxin."

The smile falls off his face, and his expression goes hard. "Shit taste in men, then."

"Agreed."

A loud beeping noise goes off in the room. Everyone around us freezes in place. and then a voice sounds over the speaker system.

"Could everyone please make their way to the exits? This is not a drill."

Hundreds of people make their way toward the doors to head outside.

"Fire alarm?" I ask Link.

"Yeah."

"You and Goat walk past the weapons room and make sure it's not left unattended before this room empties. I'm not having any of us blamed for something we didn't do."

"On it."

Link and Goat head toward the front of the room. The rest of us wait until the majority of the readers and authors have left and bring up the rear. My eyes catch a flash of red, and I see Elora taking photographs of Whitney. I think Whitney is trying to look scared, and I burst out laughing. The women turn and see me.

Whitney shrugs. "Might as well make the most of it."

Elora is smiling at her friend, and I can't get over how pretty she is when she smiles. Her hazel eyes sparkle.

"Best be heading for the door, ladies."

Elora holds up her cell phone and takes a picture

of me. "It's for Whitney."

"Sure it is," I tease.

Elora shakes her head at me, and the two of them walk in front of us and outside into the sunshine. A fire truck is pulling up as we hit the sidewalk.

"That was quick." I fold my arms across my chest.

"They must have been in the area," Elora states.

"Yeah." Leaning forward, I peer down at her cell phone. "Did you get any good pics?"

"It's hard to take a bad photo of Whit, Amazon goddess that she is." Elora flicks through her pictures as I lean in to see better.

"You're right, she looks great."

"Oh, stop it," Whitney replies with fake embarrassment. "You'll make me blush."

Elora rolls her eyes at her friend. "Yes, because you are so shy and withdrawn."

Whitney is thoughtful for a moment before she says, "I can be."

"Can't we all?" I ask.

Wolf whistles stop the conversation as the firemen enter the building, and the crowd goes crazy.

Giving Elora a wink, I move farther away from them and the crowd. It's one thing to have a table in front of you to keep the women away, but it's another to be in the middle of them as they fawn over the firemen trying to get through the crowd and see if the building is safe.

"Make way," yells an older fireman.

When I'm out of the throng of women, I stop and turn around. Whitney and Elora are right behind me.

"Whoa."

"You were our blocker to get us out of the crowd," Elora says.

Smiling, I say, "Glad I could be of service."

She tries to suppress a smile. "You're tall and large, so they all move out of the way. When you're short and petite, they tend to walk all over you."

"In that outfit, you're hard to miss. I'm sure they'd move."

Elora peers down at herself. "What does that mean?"

"It means you look good."

Her eyes travel up my body, and I'm wishing we were somewhere a little more intimate.

"Does that work?"

"What?"

Elora goes up on tip toes to appear taller. "It means you look good," she mimics my voice.

Not fazed by her bravado, I say, "You do. It's a fact."

She drops down, and her arms curl around her middle in embarrassment. Elora avoids my gaze and moves a little away from me.

"Prez," Boxer yells as he strides through the crowd, worry etched on his features. "Are you okay?"

"Yes. It's only a fire alarm. Someone probably thinks it's funny."

Boxer stands between Elora and me. "Probably."

Peering around him to Elora, I notice her head is down, and she's looking at her cell phone with Whitney. To get a better view of her, I move slightly back. Boxer frowns and gives her a once-over, disapproval evident in his frown.

"Isn't that..." Whitney asks Elora but doesn't finish her sentence.

"Yeah, sure looks like him."

Moving toward them, I ask, "Is something wrong?"

Elora swallows. "It looks like Toxin is hiding in the room."

"Show me." Elora stands next to me and flicks through the pictures. "Where?"

Starting from the beginning, she blows up the image, and sure enough, Toxin is in the background. Elora shrinks the image, and I can clearly see him walking behind a table and ducking down.

"Why?" I say out loud, more to myself.

"Do you think he pulled the fire alarm?"

Suspicion crawls up my spine. "He wanted us out of the room."

"But why?"

Breaking eye contact, I survey the crowd. Standing near the front door are the security guards. The weapons room is not protected.

"Boxer, find the Defiant Men."

"What?"

"You heard me, and if you see any of ours, send them my way."

Boxer moves into the crowd, and I stay with the two women.

"Is everything okay?" Elora asks.

"Not sure."

She touches my arm, sending a tingle all the way to my heart. "Can we do anything?"

A million thoughts crash through my brain, and all of them end up with Elora under me in bed. But she's in Defiant territory. She dated one of them. Elora is trouble.

"If you see Toxin, let me know."

Moving away from her, I head toward Goat and Link.

"Did you see Boxer?"

"Yeah. He's over there near those trees with the Defiant Men." Link points.

"Right. Let's go join him."

Walking three across, most people move, or we move around them. It takes a few minutes to get to the Defiant Men MC. They are near the fire truck, and more than one woman is getting her picture taken with a fireman with the truck in the background.

Tank, the president of the Defiant Men MC, moves toward me. Out of the corner of my eye, I see Shotgun heading over to us with three of his men.

"Grim." Tank's down-turned mouth shows his distaste for me.

"Tank." I hold out my hand, and he shakes it. "Where's Toxin?"

Tank glances around. "Here somewhere."

"Did you see him leave the building?"

The VP for the Defiant Men steps up. "What, do you think Toxin is going to do something? Get over yourself."

Tank holds up a hand. "Why?"

Ignoring his VP, I say, "Did he pull the fire alarm?"

"Why would he do that?"

"The weapons room is unattended."

Tank's eyes move to the front of the building, and he sees the security guards. "So what?"

"I'm not going down for something I didn't do."

"I know you don't like Toxin, but he's a good soldier. We all agreed to a no-violence weekend. He'll keep to his word."

"He better."

Tank's nostrils flare. "He will."

Shotgun stands next to both of us. "Gentlemen, may I suggest you move away from each other? You're making everyone nervous."

He spreads his arms wide and places a hand on each of us. Tank breaks eye contact with me and looks down at Shotgun's hand on his arm, a sneer on his face.

"I suggest you remove your hand before I take it off."

Shotgun's hands fall away. "Don't be a grumpy fucker, Tank. I'm only trying to keep the peace."

"I'm not the one accusing anyone of doing anything. Grim is."

"Fuck you, Tank. I'm only asking a question."

Tank steps up to me, and Shotgun pushes us apart.

"Do we have a problem here?" a female asks.

Sapphire Knight has her hands on her hips and a scowl on her face.

"Not from us," Tank states.

"I'm good," Shotgun says.

"Just fucking peachy," I reply.

"Need I remind you gentlemen that you made a promise? One I'm sure you're all going to keep."

With a nod, I turn around and see Toxin standing behind me.

"Hey, Grim, how goes it?" Toxin has a gleam in his eyes and confidence in his stance.

"Where were you?"

His eyebrows go up in surprise. "Out here with everyone else."

"Where exactly?"

"Last I heard, you weren't the president of my MC, so I don't answer to you." Toxin walks around me and my men to stand next to Tank.

Not wanting to be in his presence any longer than I have to, I grit my teeth and walk away from him. In truth, I want to put my gun under his chin and pull the trigger until it's empty. I want his brains all over the ground and his blood staining the earth, but now isn't the time.

Moving to stand near the security guards, I ask, "Did you clear the room before you left?"

Rex says, "I did a walk-through. There were a couple of stragglers, but the room was empty when we left."

Pointing to Toxin, I ask, "What about him? Was he out?"

The other security guard, Brett, says, "The room was empty until the firemen went in."

"So no one else came out?"

They both shake their heads.

Glowering at Toxin, the first tendrils of unease work their way up my spine. He's a sneaky fucker, and if Elora's photographs show me anything, it's that he hid in the room. The real question is, why? Was it to get to our weapons or something else?

Crossing my arms, I say to Rex, "I want to look at our weapons when we go back in."

"Is there something I should know?"

"Nope. I simply want to make sure everything is okay."

Rex looks from me to Toxin and then back to Brett. "Fine. But no one enters the room."

"Perfectly fine. I'm not about to do anything, I

just want to make sure nothing's been tampered with."

Brett barks out a laugh. "Paranoid much?"

Looking him directly in the eye, I say, "You better believe it."

Elora

Grim walked away without a backward glance, leaving Whitney and me to wonder what the hell was going on.

Why would Toxin hide in the room?

Did he pull the fire alarm?

"Penny for your thoughts?"

Smiling at Whitney, I shrug. "Thinking about Toxin."

Whitney scoffs. "Pfft, why? Honestly, if I had to choose between Toxin and Grim, I'd take Grim."

Waving a hand in her face, I say, "No, not like that. I was wondering why Toxin would want to get everyone out of the room and what he's up to. If... and it's a big *if*... I had to choose between the two of them, I'd choose... neither."

"What?" Whitney splutters.

"Bikers, remember?"

"Yeah, but Grim is nothing like Toxin."

"And you know this from what, two, maybe three conversations?"

"Hell, I knew it the minute he spoke to us."

Moving farther away from the crowd, we find ourselves at the picnic table we were at earlier. Sitting down, I look out over the people.

"They really like their books, don't they?"

Whitney sits beside me. "Yes. Are you having fun?"

Looking up at the sky, I say, "You know what? I am. It's fun."

"Did you find any books to buy?"

"Not yet."

"Do you want suggestions?"

Knowing Whitney is an avid reader and fangirling all over the place, I shake my head. "If something piques my interest, I'll buy it."

"Ask me first."

"Whit, you can't have read every book in that building. There's like one hundred authors in there."

"I've read an e-book from every one of them." My mouth falls open, and I gawk at her. "What? I'm not the only one who has. I've known about this for over twelve months. So I made a point of reading one book from every author."

"Wait, how many books is that in a month?"

"It's like ten-ish books a month. Sometimes I only read novellas for the authors I didn't know much about, but keep in mind I like MC, so I've read most of the MC authors here."

"How much do you spend on books?"

Whitney blushes. "I work so I can spend a little every week, and I'm in KU."

"KU? Is that some sort of club for readers?"

Laughing, Whitney shakes her head and then nods. "Sort of. I pay a monthly fee to Amazon, and I can read as many books as I like that are enrolled in the program. The ones I really like, I buy as well. You should try it."

"I don't read like you do."

"Reading expands your mind."

Knowing I'm not going to win, I nod. "The people here seem nice."

"Book people are the best people." Whitney sits a little straighter, and her smile grows bigger.

"You're really into this, aren't you?"

Nodding like a mad woman, she says, "Yep."

"Attention, all authors, please make your way to

the doors."

"That's Sapphire Knight," Whitney explains. "She organized this event. Sounds like the event is about to reopen."

"I guess they want the authors in first."

"Makes sense. Book people are good people, but not everyone is honest. The authors might lose books if they don't get to their tables first."

"People suck."

Whitney shrugs. "Some do, not all."

"Authors, I'm about to let readers in, so get a hustle on."

Whitney and I sit in comfortable silence, soaking up the May sunshine. My eyes are closed, and my face is raised to the sky.

"Damn, Elora, you look pretty."

Toxin's voice grates on my soul like fingernails down a chalkboard.

"What do you want, Toxin?"

"Saw you with Grim."

"And?"

"Thought you swore off bikers?"

"None of your business." I stand and throw my hair over one shoulder.

"He's bad news."

Arching one eyebrow at him, I put my hand on

my hip and glared at him.

"Readers, make your way inside. And don't forget we're selling raffle tickets for charity. Get them before they run out."

"Come on, Whit, let's get you inside."

Toxin reaches out and grabs my arm. *"Elora."*

"Take. Your. Hand. Off. Me," I grit out.

Toxin releases me. "You know you're his type. Blonde, beautiful, and trash."

Holding up my hand, I give him the finger and walk away.

Whitney laughs as she puts her arm around my shoulders. "I want to be you when I grow up."

"What... blonde, beautiful, and trash?"

"Aww... fuck him, El, you're not that. He's jealous, is all."

"He's a dick, is all. Actually, he's a walking dick who is only after one thing, and then he moves on. They're all the same."

"Men?"

"No, bikers."

"Girl, not all men are like that, so not all bikers are either. You've had man trouble with him, but it doesn't mean Grim is like Toxin."

Sighing, I say, "Whit, I love you, but can we keep my man-trouble conversation to a minimum? I'm not interested right now. To be honest, I'm thinking of quitting my job and either finding something new or studying, or both, and I think I need to move."

"Because you are in the Defiant Men MC territory?"

"Yes, but it's not the only reason. If I move a little further out of town, the rent is cheaper, so if I decide to study, I can afford to take a part-time job."

Whitney reaches for my hand. "You know, I have a friend who has some land with a tiny house on it. I could ask if they want to rent it out."

"I said out of town, not in the boonies."

Whitney laughs. "I'll ask her. The worst she can say is no."

The crowd of women and the odd man slowly reenter the venue. Whitney grabs my hand and drags me to where we were before we had to leave. Looking around the room, I can't see Grim or Toxin. Hopefully, they are both far away from me.

Grim

As I stand outside the weapons room, I notice Brett and Rex both giving me the stink eye, and neither is moving to let me inside.

"You can stand right next to me, but I have reason to believe someone has been in the weapons room. All I want to do is check my weapon."

Brett sighs and runs a hand over his shaved head. "I get it, I do, but if I let you in, I have to let everyone in. I'm not opening us up to litigation or worse from the other MCs."

He's right. If I heard another MC member had been allowed into the room, I'd be furious and demand to be allowed in.

Crossing my arms across my chest, I sigh heavily. "Could we at least look at the guns and knives on our table? You can bring them out one at a time."

Brett looks over his shoulder at our weapons. "Only the guns and knives?"

"Yeah."

Brett throws his hands in the air and moves into the room. He picks up a knife and walks it to me. It's Red's, and he's right beside me. Brett holds it out, and Red takes it off him and turns it one way and then the other.

"Looks fine to me, Prez." Red hands the knife back to Brett.

Next, he grabs my Glock and holds it out. Taking it off him, I notice the weight feels off, and it's lighter than it should be.

"It's yours, yeah?" Brett asks.

"Yeah." Cautiously, I hand it back to Brett, who retrieves another gun.

We go through this process five more times. Red and I inspect each weapon, the last being another Glock owned by Boxer. As soon as it hits my palm, I know something isn't right with mine, and the weight is definitely off.

"Thanks, man. I appreciate you indulging us."

Brett nods, closes the door, and resumes his position in front of it with his arms crossed. Red and I walk away.

"What's wrong?" he mutters.

"My gun is off... it's too light."

"Why would someone take your bullets?"

"No idea. There are no prints on them. After Hawk got arrested for robbery, I made sure to always wipe the bullets clean and use gloves. No way I'm going to jail for small-time shit."

"Yeah, 'cause you'd be stupid enough to rob a convenience store and fire off a couple of rounds at the clerk and not collect your brass."

Hawk was not the brightest member of our MC and ended up doing fifteen years in a maximum security prison.

"If the bullets are clean, what does it matter?"

"No fucking idea. But someone has tampered with it, and if I had to guess based on the photos, it has to be Toxin."

"Leave, take your gun with you. The boys and I will be good here by ourselves."

"Hey, Grim. Is everything okay?" Shotgun asks. "Saw you two at the weapons room door. Anything I should know about?"

Although Shotgun is a friend, I'm not ready to share what I know.

"Nah. Just making sure everything is still in there after the fire alarm."

He presses his lips into a thin line and narrows his eyes. "Right."

Smiling, I shrug. "You know me... overly cautious."

"Yeah, that's what I think whenever your ugly mug pops into my brain... cautious."

"You having a good time?" I ask to change the subject.

"The women here are on another level. I think I'll come back every year, even if Sapphire doesn't invite us. I've gotten at least six numbers." Shotgun chuckles. "And the best thing is, they ain't all in Texas. I'll have a bed from here to the Canadian border."

Red leans toward him and licks his lips. "Me too."

A flash of red catches my eye, and standing not fifteen feet from me is Elora.

"I'll be back."

She's got a book in her hands and is reading the back of it. Her brow is furrowed as she chews on her bottom lip. Slowly, a smile spreads across her face, and she opens her small handbag, pulling out some bills. Before she can hand over the money to the author, I thrust a twenty at her.

"Oh. That's so nice," the author gushes and hands me my change.

"Wait," Elora says.

"My way of saying thank you."

"Who would you like it made out to, honey?"

Elora scowls at me, then looks at the author. "Sorry?"

The author flushes red. "Do you want me to sign it?"

"Her name is Elora."

The author smiles widely at me, sits down, and scribbles in the front of the book. Elora holds out a twenty to me.

"It's a gift."

"I don't know you."

"Well, it's my way of getting to know you." She puts a hand on her hip and taps her foot on the floor. "How about you buy me a drink later?"

"Here you go, Elora," the author says. "Thank you so much, and I hope you like it."

Elora takes the book. "Thank you."

She thrusts it into the bag she's carrying, and I bend down to take it off her.

"I've got it." Elora moves slightly away from me.

Putting my hands in my jeans pockets, I look around for her friend Whitney. "Where's your friend?"

Elora points behind her. "Last time I checked,

she was five tables that way."

"You know it's no trouble to carry your bag."

She giggles. "You want to carry my books? What is this, high school?"

The woman is not giving me a break. It's clear she's not interested in me, and yet I keep seeking her out.

"You have a good day." Not wanting to embarrass myself any further, I head for the back of the room to where my men are.

"Hey, Prez," Boxer greets.

"Having a better time?"

"It's not so bad."

Link and Goat are here.

"I need to get into the weapons room without being seen."

"Another fire alarm?" Goat asks.

"Nah, too obvious," Link states.

Boxer looks up and smirks. "Air-conditioning vent." He looks me over. "No way you're getting in a vent." Boxer taps his chin. "Hell, all of us are too big. We need someone little."

"Grim?"

Turning around, I notice Whitney standing there with two bags laden with books.

"Hey. Where's your friend?" Boxer asks as he

pulls out a chair for her.

"Elora? She's not far away."

Boxer slaps my arm. "She sure is petite."

Subtle he is not.

Whitney sits. "Thanks so much. My arms are sore from carrying so many books."

Turning a chair around, I straddle it, resting my arms on the back. "Did you want to leave them here and pick them up at the end of the day?"

Whitney nods. "You don't mind?"

"No, and there's always one of us here, so they'd be safe."

Whitney pulls all the books out of her bags and puts them on the table. Elora is walking toward us and rolls her eyes. The woman clearly doesn't like me.

"Whit, what are you doing?"

"I'm leaving the books here and picking them up at the end of the day."

"Surely you can't have many more to pick up?" Elora puts a bag of books on the table.

"A few more."

"This is only some of them," she says to me. "Whit has already put two loads in the car."

Ignoring her with a flick of her hand, Whitney says, "I did my preorders a year ago. I've been paying them off. All I have to do is pick them up."

"Then how come I see you paying for books?"

Whitney squirms in her seat. "Because some of them are limited edition covers, or they've released more books." She scrunches her nose up at Elora. "Don't you have something to say to Grim?"

Elora fixes her eyes on me. "Right." She chews on her bottom lip. "Thank you for buying me the book. It was nice of you, and I didn't need to be a bitch about it."

"It was my way of saying thank you for the photos you sent of Toxin."

Her pretty face screws up in a snarl. "He's such a dick."

"Yes, he is," Boxer says. "Here, take my seat."

Elora sits next to me and offers Boxer a smile. He raises his eyebrows at me and looks at her. Elora notices the exchange and frowns.

"Boxer, can you do a walk-around?"

"Sure can." He winks at me and strolls away.

"He's weird."

"Elora," Whitney chastises.

Laughing, I say, "Yep, he can be. The man has a way of doing things, but he's loyal to me and the club. Boxer is one of my best."

"Is that why he's here today?" Elora asks.

Smiling, I say, "Yes and no. I knew the other MCs would be here, and we don't exactly get along with the Defiant Men, so I picked the largest men in my MC to come with me."

Elora takes note of Link and Goat. "Yeah, I can see that." She leans in and whispers, "But you're the biggest."

Laughing, I relax and say, "Yep. How tall are you?"

Elora sits a little straighter on the chair. "Five foot."

"Good things come in small packages." Whitney giggles. "Sometimes she does have a Napoleon complex." I frown and tilt my head toward her. "You know, she sometimes tries to prove she's right. Little person syndrome."

"I do not."

"Yes, you do," Whitney teases her friend.

Elora huffs at her. "What time is it?"

"Lunchtime," I say.

"Do you get a lunch break?"

It's nice to be having a conversation with her and not a hostile one. "Yes. The event is providing us with sandwiches, chips, and a drink."

Elora asks Whitney, "Do you want to go and get something to eat?"

"I could eat."

Elora stands. "Do you want me to get you anything?"

After reaching into my pocket, I pull out a five-dollar bill. "A can of soda? Coke?"

Elora shakes her head. "Your money's no good here."

Smiling, I slip the money into my jeans. "Thanks, and take your time."

Elora

Begrudgingly, I have to admit I'm having a good time. The idea of spending a day at a book event isn't something I thought I'd be interested in, but here I am with a book of my own. And I'm spending time with a biker, and he hasn't tried to touch my ass or hit on me. *Maybe they aren't all the same after all?*

"Elora?" Cherry calls, walking toward me. She's a club girl, always has been. Her mother was in the life, going from biker to biker and eventually had Cherry. Rumor has it she was sold to Tank, the Defiant Men MC's president.

"Hey, Cherry."

"You here with Toxin?"

"Fuck no."

Cherry arches one perfectly manicured eyebrow, her ruby-red lips turn down, and she cocks her head to the side, studying me.

"We broke up ages ago."

"Really? He talks about you from time to time."

"Not sure what he'd say about me apart from the fact he likes to fuck around."

Cherry nods. "Men think they rule, but it's really the women who steer them. Good for you for walking away." Cherry steps closer to me and lowers her voice. "Although, he wouldn't like it."

"Tough. We're done. I've told him. I don't do cheaters, and I can't believe I fell for his bullshit."

Cherry looks around the room. "Can you believe this? All these women wishing they were us."

"I'm not in the MC, *you* are. How's Tank?"

Her face drops, Cherry's gaze firmly on the floor. "Here somewhere."

"Trouble in paradise?"

Cherry peers at me through her long, dark lashes. "Yeah. He wants to claim me."

"I thought he already had."

She straightens up, throws her red hair over one shoulder, and shrugs. "Sort of."

"Everyone thinks you're a couple. Well, that was the gossip with the other women."

"And the whores love to gossip." Cherry grits her teeth in a grimace. "The Defiant Men make a show of it when they make you an old lady."

"What do you mean?"

"He gets to fuck me in front of the entire clubhouse and then tattoo his name on my chest so everyone knows who I belong to."

Shock races through my system as I think of the number of women in the clubhouse I saw with men's names tattooed on their chests. Five maybe six? And all of them got violated in front of everyone.

Reaching out, I touch her arm, but Cherry shrinks away from me. "I don't want or need your pity."

"I didn't know. Do all MCs do this?"

Cherry shakes her head, her long hair cascading around her face. "No. The Defiant Men think it sets them apart from the other MCs. Keeps their women in line." She shrugs. "Tank thinks he loves me and wants to prove it to all of the brotherhood."

"What do you want?"

Cherry gives me a withering look. "Does it matter?"

Tucking some of my blonde hair behind one ear, I close the gap between us. "It does to me. If you need help, all you need to do is ask."

"You were smart, Elora, you escaped. Don't go troubling yourself with me. Enjoy your day." Her face morphs into a mask of happiness. "Seems like you know what you want."

With that, she walks through the crowd, and I'm struck by how alone she is. It's funny how we can see someone and assume they are exactly where they want to be when, all along, they're trapped.

"You okay?" Whitney is next to me with another book in her hands.

"Do you know Cherry?"

"I've seen her around. She belongs to Tank, right?"

"Yeah, but I don't think she wants to."

Whitney shrugs. "She made her bed."

"I'm not sure she did. When I was with Toxin, the other girls talked about her mother and not in a nice way. Cherry grew up around the clubs, but her mother was well-known for being a whore. Apart from Tank, I don't think Cherry got passed around."

"Well, she's Tank's woman. Pretty much a club princess."

"More like a queen. None of the other members touch her. Not a hand. Tank watches her with eagle eyes."

"And her mother?" Whitney puts the book into a bag.

"The other club girls told me she disappeared around the time Cherry was given to Tank." Whitney nods. "Did you know when they claim a woman, they have sex with her in front of the entire MC and then tattoo their name on her chest?"

Whitney gives me the side-eye. "Surely not?"

"Cherry told me."

"Well, you dodged a bullet then, didn't you?"

I laugh. "I was never going to marry Toxin. There are too many things I want to do."

"Like what?" Grim asks, appearing beside me with a brown paper bag in his hands.

"Are you stalking me?"

He grins. "I was looking for you. Does that count as stalking?" He holds up the bag. "I got lunch, so I thought I'd join you."

"I'm going to leave you two to it. I want to go and talk to Nicole James while her line is short." Whitney hands me the book she's holding. "I'll find you at the café."

"She's right into all of this, isn't she?" Grim falls into step beside me.

"Yeah, I had no idea she read this much. She's read a book from every author here."

"Is it cool if I join you?"

"Sure."

Grim and I walk together into the café in the venue. He pulls a chair out for me and then sits down. His mother taught him right.

A server comes over. "Hey, folks, what can I get you?"

"For the moment, two Cokes and a menu?"

The woman looks at me and then down at the table. "I'm so sorry. We are swamped today. There should be a menu on the table." Turning, she grabs one off the table next to us. "I'll get your drinks while you decide. Sorry about that."

"All good."

Grim opens his brown paper bag and frowns. "Multigrain bread."

"You don't like it?"

"Nah. Is there anything healthy on the menu?"

Scanning the menu, I say, "There's a chicken cobb salad. So, you're a health nut?"

One side of his mouth turns down. "Yes and no. My brother died from cancer, so I try to live cleanly… most of the time."

"Aah, I'm sensing you have weaknesses." I cock an eyebrow and nod sagely at him.

Grim chuckles. "I can't pass up a hot fudge

sundae and the odd Shiner Bock."

"You rebel you." I flutter my eyelashes at him and giggle.

"How about you? Any vices I should know about?"

My lips turn down, and I look up at the ceiling, thinking. "Chocolate, and I drink way too much coffee."

Grim leans to the side and looks me up and down. "Doesn't look like you indulge too much."

Blushing, I shift uncomfortably in my seat. "I work out like a demon. Otherwise, my ass could have a postcode of its own."

Grim laughs loudly, his brown eyes sparkling in the light. "I'm sure that's not true."

Our server comes back with two Cokes. "Have you decided what you'd like?"

"Two chicken cobb salads, please."

"Should we get something for Whitney?" Grim asks.

"Yeah." I look up at the server. "Make that three chicken cobb salads and a bottle of water, please."

"Could you make it two bottles of water?"

"Sure can." She writes on her pad and scurries away.

Grim links his fingers together on the table, and

I notice the many tattoos he has on his hands and arms. His black T-shirt strains against his muscles.

"Are all your tattoos black and gray?"

He points to his wrist and the red flowers that are covered by some chunky silver bracelets. "Mostly, but I have the odd bit of red here and there. Do you have any tattoos?"

"I've got a rose in American traditional on my back and some script on my ribs."

Grim pulls up the sleeve of his shirt, showing me more of his arm. "I've got some script too."

The words 'love,' 'hate,' and 'pain' are written on his bicep in thick lettering. They almost look like a cover-up, as I can see a pattern behind them.

"Nice."

Grim shrugs and pulls his shirt down. "Club life... sometimes you do stupid shit."

"Have you always been in?"

"Yeah, sort of the family business. Have you always lived in Defiant Men territory?"

Leaning back in my chair, I shake my head. "I didn't know it was their territory when I moved there. I got a job at Bobby's Bar and didn't want a long commute."

"Makes sense."

"Yeah, but I'm thinking of moving and changing jobs."

Grim studies me for a moment before he asks, "Where are you thinking of moving to and what kind of job?"

After taking a deep breath, I exhale slowly. "Somewhere cheaper if there is such a thing, and I like the idea of helping people."

"Isn't that what bartenders do?"

Giggling, I nod. "Yeah, but it would be nice to help sober people."

The server returns with the waters. "Here you go. Your meals shouldn't be far behind."

Glancing around the café, I notice it's packed. Our server looks like she's frazzled, and her brown hair is falling out of her ponytail.

"How did you get involved with an author signing?"

Grim rubs his eyes. "Sapphire Knight's husband, Jamie, is a friend. I owed him a favor. So, here we are." He leans forward and lowers his voice. "And 'cause we are local, it's good for us to be seen doing something nice. MCs don't generally have a good name in Texas. I thought this might help."

"Excuse me, ma'am, is this man bothering you?"

Standing next to our table is a marshal. He's got

one hand on his hip, holding back his jacket so we can see his badge clipped to his belt. He'd be good-looking if it weren't for the sneer on his face as he stares down at Grim.

"No, sir. We're having lunch."

"You often have lunch with felons?"

Grim stands, towering over the marshal. "Why don't you fuck off, Johnny?"

"That's Marshal to you."

Like a pair of gorillas, they stand close to each other, chests almost touching. Grim is taller than the marshal by a good six or seven inches, but the lawman isn't backing down.

"Can you smell that?" I ask, looking around the café.

I wait until both men are looking at me.

"Can you?" I ask again.

"What?" the marshal asks as he takes a deep breath.

"The male testosterone in this room is overwhelming." I stand, putting my hands on my hips. "I know some women find it sexy, but me... nah, it's stupid, childish, and a turn-off."

Grim laughs, but the marshal looks pissed. His face flushes as he looks me up and down then strides out of the café without a backward glance.

"Who the hell was he?"

"Marshal Johnny Saint-Mark."

"Did you piss in his Froot Loops?"

Grim laughs louder and sits down. "He has a thing for bikers."

"No, that can't be it. There are over a dozen of you here, and he singled you out. So tell me."

Grim looks to his left, head bent, then slowly moves his eyes to me again. "One of his brethren got caught in a gunfight. Johnny and I used to be friends about a million years ago, but when that happened, I became public enemy number one."

"Was it your fault?"

"No. But I'm where he focused his rage. Marshal Johnny Saint-Mark takes every opportunity to ruin my day if he can."

"If you were friends, have you tried talking to him?"

Grim sucks in a breath. "We took different paths. The thing is..." he taps the table, "... I was always going to go into this life. It's where I belong, and I guess being a lawman is where he belongs."

"I feel like you're not telling me everything."

Grim sits back, eyebrows raised. "Well, Elora, this is our first date, and I don't want it to be too serious."

A giggle escapes me. "Date?"

"We're sitting at a table, I'm buying you lunch, and we're talking. Sounds like a date to me."

His smirk is cute, and I know he's teasing me, but there's an edge of truth to his words.

"Hey, you two. Have you eaten?" Whitney asks as she sits down.

Breaking eye contact with Grim, I can't help the smile that crosses my face. "We've ordered. You got a water and a chicken cobb salad."

"Damn, girl, Grim is good for you. You ordered something other than pizza."

"They don't have pizza."

Grim chuckles, and our server returns with our meals. "Here you go. Can I get you folks anything else?"

"No, thanks, we're good." Grim winks at her. She blushes and hurries away.

"Is that all you have to do... flash a smile and a wink, and they all fall at your feet?" My words come out a little more harshly than I intend. Seeing him flirt with the server annoyed me, maybe even making me a tad jealous.

Grim shakes his head. "I was only being friendly. She's run off her feet... a little kindness goes a long way."

Whitney hands me a fork, and I stab it into my salad. Now I feel like an asshole.

"Did you get any more books?"

Whit bounces up and down in her seat. "You know I did." She holds up three more books. "Got these off Nicole James." She looks at Grim. "Do you read?"

"Yeah, but not romance. I like short stories, mainly science fiction. Have you heard of Isaac Asimov?"

Whitney shakes her head. "No."

"Well, he's been dead a good long while, but they made some of his works into movies. *I, Robot*, *Bicentennial Man*. Ring any bells?"

Whitney nods, and I stare at him blankly.

"You don't read?" Grim stares into my eyes.

"Sometimes."

"What do you like?"

Feeling as though I'm being judged, I shrug. "Aah, well..."

"She's still finding her groove," Whitney answers for me. "This cobb salad is one of the best I've ever had. How's yours, Grim?"

"It's good." He takes a forkful of salad and puts it in his mouth.

We sit in uncomfortable silence for a while, each

of us eating. Whitney gives me large eyes when Grim isn't looking, and I give her a small smile. This does not comfort her, and she reaches under the table and squeezes my leg.

"Do you have many more authors to see?" My voice comes out squeaky and rushed.

"Yeah, a few. I've only done half of the room."

"Are you going tonight?" Grim asks.

"No, I didn't get tickets."

"Tickets to what?" I ask.

"There's a dinner on," Whitney tells me. "I couldn't afford the tickets."

"I happen to have a spare," Grim says between mouthfuls.

Whitney's mouth drops open, but she quickly closes it. "Only one?"

"I could probably wrangle two."

"Oh my God, oh my God, oh my God." Whitney grabs my hand. "What are we going to wear?"

"We?"

"Yes, we. You don't think I'd leave you and go alone, do you?" Whitney pulls out her cell phone from her bag. "I've gotta check with Tony to make sure this is okay. I'll be right back."

She rushes out of the café, and I ask Grim, "What did you do?"

"Got you and your friend tickets to tonight?" He's smiling and clearly happy with himself.

"Grim, I'm not a reader. I don't know any of these people. I only came today because Whit is a friend, and I'm a lousy friend."

"So... you don't want to go?"

"No, but now I have to."

"I'm going. It's being held in a bar close to my clubhouse. They make great burgers."

"*Great.*"

"It starts at seven, and Sapphire said it should all be over by ten."

"Yeah, 'cause on my one weekend off in forever I want to hang out at a bar."

"Sorry." Grim looks down at his salad, and I feel like a bitch.

"No, I'm sorry. You're doing something nice, and once again, I'm not handling it well. It's just I had plans for a long soak, paint my nails, maybe even a glass of bubbles. Now, I'm in heels, a dress, and a dinner in a bar."

Grim pushes his salad away and rests his elbows on the table. "How can I fix this?"

"Are you going?"

"Yes."

"Okay, do you want to take me?"

He looks confused. "Yes?"

"No, I mean it as in an actual date. You pick me up, you drop me home, and no getting past first base."

Grim shakes his head. "Did you ask me out?"

"No, *you're* taking *me* out."

Grim grins at me. "It's a *date*."

Grim

Walking back into the venue, Boxer rushes up to me. "So, did you ask her?"

"No."

"Why not?"

Moving through the crowd, I hold a finger up to silence him. When we make it to our table, it's surrounded by women posing with Link and Goat for photographs. Quickly, I turn around and walk in the opposite direction. There's a sign for restrooms, so I make a beeline for it. Once inside, I check all the stalls to make sure it's empty.

"I like her."

"What?"

"Elora... I like her. *And* I hardly know her."

"I don't understand." Boxer puts a hand on the

back of his head and rubs. "I get you like her, but why not ask her?"

"She's different, and she also has sworn off bikers as she thinks we're all scum. I don't want her thinking I'm like every other douche she's dated. So, asking her to break into a room is out of the question."

"You're not asking her to take anything. Just swap things around a little. Your gun is clean… we know this. No bodies on it. Tank's, we have no fucking idea. Hell, he could have killed a dozen people. You're the one taking the risk, not Tank."

"But Elora doesn't know that. She could think we're setting him up."

"So tell her we aren't." I narrow my eyes at Boxer, and he throws an arm in the air. "For fuck's sake, Grim. Elora is the one who showed you the photos of Toxin hiding in the room during the fire alarm. Spell it out for her. The worst that can happen is she'll say no."

"No, Boxer, the worst that can happen is she'll tell Toxin or Tank."

This stops him. He puts both hands on his hips and looks down at the floor. Raising his head, he regards me, his lips turned down.

"Yeah. It'd fuck up everything." He tilts his head

from side to side. "Still worth the risk."

The door to the restroom opens, and a guy dressed in leathers walks in. He's covered in tattoos but doesn't have colors on, so he must be one of the male models. He smiles broadly at us and enters one of the stalls.

Boxer raises his eyebrows and smirks at me. I shake my head and walk outside.

"What the fuck was that?"

"A model. Have you even looked at some of the book covers? They've got tattooed men in biker outfits."

Boxer looks me up and down. "You could be on one of those covers."

A woman stops and looks at Boxer. "Oh, honey, *you* could be too." She winks at him and keeps going.

Boxer goes a shade of red. I've never seen him blush before. Laughing, I walk through the crowd and head to our table.

Walking outside to a vending machine, I put in my money and hit the button for a Sprite.

"Figured you for a Coke man."

Elora is searching through her tiny handbag for change.

"I've got it. What do you want?" I ask as I feed the machine.

"Coke, and thank you."

The can noisily drops out of the machine, and I retrieve it for her. "Most days, it's water, but today I felt like this." I hold up my Sprite.

"Are you and Whitney still having a good time?"

"Whitney is in heaven. And even though this isn't my thing, it's been fun."

"Well, aren't you two cozy?" Toxin sidles up to the vending machine and winks at Elora. "Didn't take you long to move on, did it?"

Elora rolls her eyes. "What do you want?"

Toxin points at a Coke logo. "Same as you. See, we have so much in common."

"No, we don't." Venom drips from Elora's words.

"Toxin, why don't you take a hint and leave the lady alone?"

Toxin chuckles and points at me. "Don't you know, Grim? She's no lady."

Before I can react, Elora steps forward and punches him in the face. Toxin's head bounces off the vending machine, making a satisfying thud.

Wrapping my arms around Elora, who kicks and thrashes like a wild cat, I move her further away from Toxin. He scowls at us, rubbing his jaw.

"You're lucky Grim is here, or I'd repay you for that."

"Fuck you. Grim, let me go."

"Not until you calm down." Toxin walks toward me. "If you take another step, I will let her go, and then you'll have me *and* Elora to answer to. Walk away."

Toxin's face contorts with frustration as he slowly turns and walks away. His fists are clenched at his sides, and his shoulders are bunched in an effort to hold himself back. Toxin casts a longing glance over his shoulder, his eyes burning with anger.

"You'll get yours, Grim."

Deep down, I'm unhappy I don't get to fight Toxin. Elora is my only concern. She's no longer thrashing around, and I release her. If Toxin and I had come to blows, she most certainly would have gotten in the middle and possibly hurt.

"What the fuck?" Elora's face is twisted with anger.

She takes a deep breath and exhales, some of the tension visibly leaving her body. Her gaze follows

Toxin as he walks into the venue.

"Are you okay?"

"That was stupid. I shouldn't have lashed out." Elora sighs. "Just so you know, I'm not a slut. I... I don't want you thinking badly of me."

My heart is pounding in my chest. "I need to tell you something." Elora holds eye contact. "I like you. It blows my mind you were with Toxin. He's a fucking idiot, but we all make mistakes."

Elora looks surprised and a little bit pleased. She smiles warmly at me, and I feel a rush of relief she's not rejecting me.

"I like you too."

Smiling back at her, I tease, "Even though I'm in an MC? The very type of male you declared you'd never date again?"

"You're nothing like him." Elora's brow furrows, and she squints at me. "I was wrong to put all bikers in one box."

"Sounds like we have the beginnings of a beautiful friendship."

She purses her lips. "We could cement this newfound friendship by killing Toxin. What do you think?"

I know she's teasing me, but here goes nothing. "Elora, I have a favor to ask. It involves Toxin."

"Is it illegal?"

"Not really?"

Elora opens her can of soda. "Ask me, but I might not say yes."

"Fair enough." I open my Sprite and take a sip. "My gun in the weapons room doesn't feel right. It's light."

"You think Toxin has done something to it?"

"Yes."

Elora takes a few steps away, then looks at me and tips her head, indicating I should follow.

"What do you want me to do?"

"Climb in through the air-conditioning vent and swap my gun for someone else's on the Defiant Men's table."

She stops walking. Her mouth is open, and she quickly snaps it shut. "No."

"If you're worried about someone getting in trouble, my gun is clean. No bodies, no hold-ups. It's my personal gun. I use it for protection."

"Still no."

Even though I understand why Elora is saying no, I'm still disappointed. She takes a sip of her soda and looks past me. Her eyes widen, and she takes a step back. Turning, I see Tank barreling toward us.

Without thinking twice, I move in front of Elora,

shielding her from Tank's thunderous gaze. Standing tall, my eyes focus on him as he draws closer. My heart pounds in my chest, but outwardly, I appear calm. I'm the only thing standing between Elora and one pissed-off biker. Adrenaline surges through me as Tank approaches. He's not getting past me. I'll protect Elora, no matter what.

"Stop there, Tank," I say firmly.

"She hit one of my men."

Holding my hands out, I shrug. "He deserved it."

Tank frowns, and behind him, I can see more of his men coming toward us.

"Grim, how would you feel if a woman lashed out at one of your men?"

"I'd ask the lady why."

Tank's head whips back in surprise. "Fine." Tank looks around me at Elora. "Why'd you punch Toxin?"

"He's been baiting me all day. He keeps calling me on different numbers, and I've had to block each and every one of them. I want nothing to do with him, but the man can't take a hint."

"And?" Tank demands.

"And he basically called me a slut. I am not."

The tension between the two of them is palpable. Taking a deep breath, I step forward, hands raised in a calming gesture.

In a soft, measured tone, I say, "You know how he can be." I dip my head at the incoming men. "It's not worth starting a war over. Call your men off. Elora will keep away from Toxin. All you need to do is keep him away from her. He started it, not her."

Tank's mouth goes into a hard line. He takes a deep breath, his nostrils flare, and just as I think he's about to come at me swinging, he says, "Don't let her near him again." Tank turns around, his men flanking him, then holds up a finger and makes a circle in the air, showing they should leave as well. "Elora?" Tank says loudly, still facing away from us.

"Yeah?" she says, peeking out from behind me.

"Don't do it again. You have this one free pass, there won't be another. Understood?"

Elora moves to stand beside me. "I understand."

Tank nods and stalks back the way he came, with his men following close behind. I clench and unclench my fist, trying to release some of the tension in my body.

"Grim?"

"Yeah?"

"I'm in."

Elora

Here I am on my hands and knees, crawling through an air-conditioning duct for a man I hardly know.

What the hell is wrong with me?

Sure, he's good-looking, and yes, he appears to be a nice guy, but don't they all start out that way? And all because I didn't like the way Tank was prepared to whip my ass for Toxin.

Looking through the grate below me, I see the inside of the weapons room. It flips down easily, and I poke my head through. There's no one in the room. The opening is above a closet, and I crawl out onto the top of it. I'm lucky there isn't a huge drop, or I'd be able to get in the room but not out. From the top of the closet, I drop down onto the carpeted floor. Moving quickly toward the tables, I find the

Warriors of Destruction table, and after picking up three different guns, I find Grim's with his paperwork under it.

My daddy taught me how to use a gun, so I'm not scared of them, but holding one in my hand feels unnatural. It's been a while since I've fired one. Searching the other tables, I find the Defiant Men's weapons and eventually Tank's gun. I pick it up and inspect it. There's nothing distinguishable that would make him think it's not his. I put Grim's in its place and put his on top of Grim's paperwork. Yeah, I picked Tank's after his macho bullshit outside. If something is wrong with Grim's gun, it's fitting Tank should suffer the consequences.

Sweat drips between my breasts as my nerves get the best of me. If someone walks into this room, I'm as good as dead.

There's no way I can climb to the top of the closet on my own, so I move a chair next to it. Hopefully, no one will notice the chair has been moved. I take less than a minute to get back up into the air-conditioning vent and crawl back to Grim.

Dangling my legs through the hole, I feel his hand touch my foot, so I lower myself. His muscular arms encircle me as he lowers me to the floor.

"Are you okay?"

Still in his arms, I look at my filthy hands. "I'm dirty."

Grim chuckles and lets me go. "So are your jeans."

Looking down, my knees are black, and so are the tops of my bare feet. "Yuck."

"We need to get you cleaned up."

"I should have taken off my jeans when I took off my red top."

"Too late now. Did you do it?"

"Yes."

He grabs my face and kisses the top of my head. "Thank you. I owe you for this."

"You're paying for dinner *and* drinks."

He laughs into my hair, then steps away. "But I'm not getting past first base?"

Grim is teasing me, but right now, he could kiss me, and I'm not sure I'd have the presence of mind to stop him. There's something about a man being able to hold me and make me feel safe.

Safe.

Yeah, Grim makes me feel safe. It's not only his size—it's everything he does. Every conversation where I've tested him and he's comforted me, or at least tried to has put me at ease.

"Now what?"

"We need to get you out of here without anyone seeing you like this. Put your shirt and shoes on, walk behind me as close as you can, and I'll take you out a side door."

He opens the door to the room we are in, and I put a hand under his cut, touching his T-shirt. His back feels warm and hard.

"What were you two doing in there?"

Looking around his large frame, Toxin is standing there. He frowns when he sees me.

"Wow, Elora, you didn't make him wait long, did you?"

Grim puts a hand to his chest, pushing him out of the way. "Fuck off, Toxin. It's none of your business."

"She's *my* business."

Grim faces him. "Not. Any. More."

Reaching down, Grim grabs my hand and puts me in front of him as he hustles me out a side door. Grim pulls me along until we get to his bike. He unclips a helmet and hands it to me.

"You've been on the back of a bike before?"

"Yes, I used to ride." I put the helmet over my head.

Grim climbs on and holds out a hand to me. Ignoring it, I place a hand on his shoulder and hop on the bike.

He looks over his shoulder at me and smiles. "Hang on."

The bike comes to life, and he pulls out of the parking lot and onto the road. When I want him to turn, I tap his shoulder, and he turns the bike. When we are close to my home, I tap in the middle of his back, and he pulls over.

"This is me." I point at my apartment.

Grim parks in the visitor parking, turns the engine off, and waits for me to dismount.

After taking off the helmet, I hold it out to him. "Thanks for the ride."

"My pleasure."

"I'm going to go shower and change. Did you want to come up?"

Grim gets off the bike. "Sure."

He follows me to my apartment, and I'm nervous. My hands are sweating, and I feel like a teenager bringing home her boyfriend for the first time. After unlocking the front door, I step into my living room, and Grim follows.

"Don't go into the kitchen, it's full of dirty dishes."

Grim chuckles as he looks around my home. "I'm not here to judge you or your home."

"Okay. Well, the kitchen is there." I point in its direction. "TV, bathroom, my room. Help yourself to anything in the fridge. I'll be right back."

Looking over my shoulder, I notice Grim is watching me walk away, a smile on his lips. My insides melt a little at the tender expression on his face, but I keep going. He's in Defiant territory and unarmed without his MC to look out for him. Simply being here could be dangerous for him.

Opening my closet, I pull out another pair of jeans and a red cowl-necked tank top that drapes beautifully at the front. It makes my breasts appear bigger than they are, and I know I look good in it.

Leaving them on the bed, I pick up another bra and a pair of panties and hurry into the bathroom. One reason I rented this apartment was the shower over the bath. It makes the shower feel bigger, it's easy to shave my legs, and there's plenty of room to move around. Turning on the water, I strip out of my dirty clothes and pick up a scrubbing brush. The dirt comes off easily, but I scrub the tops of my feet and the palms of my hands.

Lathering up a loofah, I scrub myself, making sure I don't get my hair wet. When I'm done, I dry myself off and use a washcloth to wipe the steam from the mirror. Thankfully, there's no dirt on my face. After wrapping a towel around myself, I poke my head out of the bathroom, but I don't see Grim. Grateful, I dash into my bedroom and shut the door.

As quickly as I can, I dress, use my hair dryer to tame my hair, reapply some lipstick, and move to the living room. Grim isn't watching television. He's in my kitchen, and he smiles when he sees me.

"What are you doing?"

"You had some dirty dishes, so I washed them for you."

A man who does housework without being asked? My inner bitch is instantly on the defense. He's a little too good to be true.

"Do you normally do housework?"

"Hell no. There's always a club whore..." Grim stops speaking and holds up a hand. "Let me rephrase. There's always a female in the house who does housework. We also have a dishwasher."

"You live full-time at the clubhouse?"

"Yeah."

"Do these other *females* do anything else for you?"

Grim leans on the kitchen bench and crosses his arms. "They do lots of other stuff for lots of brothers in the MC."

"But you specifically?"

"Are you trying to ask me something, Elora?"

"Yes. No." Twisting my lips to the side, I drop my gaze to the floor. "A-are you... close with any of the women in the clubhouse?"

Grim moves to stand in front of me, and using two fingers, lifts my face so I'm peering up at him.

"I'm no saint. We've all got pasts, but when I'm with someone, I'm with them." His thumb traces my jawline. "I don't fuck around." He drops his hand from my face and takes a step away. "It's also been a long time since I've been exclusive. I'm the president of my MC, and it takes up a lot of my time."

My skin burns where he touched me. It feels like I've been branded. The man towers above me, all muscle and strength. Closing the gap between us, I place a hand on his chest and snake the other around his neck.

"Elora?"

"Shut up. I'm trying to be sexy."

Grim's mouth crashes into mine. This isn't soft—it's all-encompassing and passion on another level. He lifts me like I weigh nothing and puts my ass on the kitchen bench. His body goes between my thighs as his hands stroke the soft skin of my lower back. A growl escapes him when my tongue teases his.

Crushing myself against him, I glide my hands under his shirt and wrap one of my legs around his waist. His skin feels hot against the palms of my hands as I dig my fingernails into him. Grim breaks the kiss and arches his neck, and a hiss comes out of him. My lips lock onto his neck, and I drag my teeth across the flesh there.

"Fuck yes," he all but whispers.

Feeling brave, I move my hands from his back to the hard muscles of his stomach. Grim grasps my face, his eyes wide open as he kisses me. It almost feels like he's searching my soul as his tongue caresses mine. The electricity between us feels palpable like a spark has been ignited between us. One I don't want to end. Grim tastes sweet, and his scent is a mix of musk, spice, and all man.

When we finally pull apart, we're both breathless. Our eyes are locked together in a moment of intimacy. This feels like the beginning of something magical.

His hand cups the side of my face. "We should leave."

"Oh." Suddenly, it doesn't feel very magical.

"Not oh. It's not safe for me here. And as much as I want you, we haven't even had a first date. You seem like the kind of woman who plays it a lot safer than sex on the first date. Not that I'd be complaining if you broke a rule or two, but, Elora, I like you, and I haven't liked someone in a very long time."

His words sink in, and I realize he's letting me steer this relationship. It can't always be for a man like Grim, who's always in charge.

"I like you too."

His lips turn up in a smile, and he lowers his head to my forehead, brushing his lips against mine. After sweeping the hair off my neck, he peppers kisses from my jaw to my collarbone. His teeth graze my soft skin, and I gasp as he makes his way to my mouth again. I drag my fingers down his stomach to the top of his jeans, and he groans.

Like before, he breaks the kiss. He grabs my hand and presses his forehead to mine again. "Do you want this now?"

My head is fuzzy with desire, and all I want is him. Screw all my stupid rules. I want to know what it's like to have this man inside me, to see if he can take me over the edge.

"Elora?"

"Can't we keep going and see where this ends?"

Grim steps away, one hand going to the back of

his head and the other scrubbing down his face. "Arrghhh." He groans. "I've wanted you from the first moment I saw you, but you... you've been pushing me away all day. This won't be a onetime thing for me. Elora, if we keep going, I'm going to claim you."

Images of Cherry pop into my head of her being fucked in front of a room full of bikers and then, like a piece of meat, having his name branded onto her chest like property.

My legs snap closed, and I jump off the bench. "Nope."

"Wait. What happened?"

"How do you claim your women?"

He looks surprised as his mouth drops open. "What?"

"The Defiant Men fuck them in front of the clubhouse members and then tattoo their names on the chest of the one they take possession of."

Grim shakes his head. "I am *nothing* like Toxin. My club is nothing like theirs. When I claim you, I'll make it known you belong to me and no one is to touch you. No public fucking, no tattooing... just you and me alone in a room having fun. If you want to and *only* if you do."

His eyes bore into mine, and I know he's telling

the truth.

"Seems I have a habit of pissing you off."

"You do keep me on my toes."

Reaching out, I put both of my hands on his chest. "For the record, I know you're not like Toxin. It'd be like comparing chalk and cheese."

Grim covers my hands with his. "We should get back."

"Yeah." He threads his finger through mine and pulls me toward the front door. "Wait, I need my bag."

Letting him go, I rush into my bedroom, picking it up from where I left it on my bed and slinging it across my body. When I turn around, Grim is standing in the doorway, leaning against the frame.

"You should put a leather jacket on."

Opening my closet, I pull out a black leather jacket with pointy silver studs across the shoulders. When I put it on, Grim smiles.

"You know, I think that's the first time you've done what I asked without an argument."

"Makes sense. Bare arms sliding down the asphalt won't look so pretty the next day."

Grim waves a hand around my room. "I like your bedroom."

The room is painted a soft dove-gray color with

white trim. My bedspread is navy with white and gold thread running through it. It reminds me of water.

"I like it too."

"Not very girly."

Laughing, I walk toward him. "Girls can't like blue?"

"It's not only that. It's very... uncluttered?"

"So women have pink rooms and lots of shit?"

Grim takes my hand. "Come on, I can see I'm digging myself another hole."

Laughing, I let him pull me through my home and outside. "Nah, I'm only teasing you. If it makes you feel better, I collect crystal vases, bowls, and glasses."

"Good to know."

"But not figurines. Those are dust collectors. I like things I can use."

"Also good to know." When we get to his bike, he pulls out his cell phone and checks the time. "We should get there just in time for the event to close."

"And then dinner and drinks, yeah?"

Grim grins. "Yeah, I think I promised you."

Toxin

The room is practically empty. Most of the authors are packing up. Tank is pacing back and forth, always on the lookout for his woman. Cherry is his trophy, and if anyone so much as looks at her, he busts them in the face with his fist or whatever happens to be in his hand.

Subconsciously, my hand traces the scar on my hairline where he cracked me over the head with a bottle for smiling at her. No woman is worth all the shit he goes through. Every man in the club can tell she would rather be anywhere else but with him or us. Her mother, Roxy, sold her to Tank long ago. Hell, she must have been barely in her teens. Roxy got a house and money in Colorado. All she had to do was deliver her only child to Tank, whole and untouched when she turned sixteen.

I often wonder why Cherry hasn't disappeared. She's been with Tank for five years. In all that time, she could have run but didn't. Even now, as she walks toward him, a fake smile on her lips, I can tell she's not happy. Tank doesn't seem to notice. Cherry is his property, and he's keeping her.

"Brother, you'd best drop your gaze, or Tank will catch you looking." Randy is standing next to me, a slight smile on his lips. "I get it. She's hot but not worth the stitches. How many did you get last time?"

"Twenty-three."

His lips pucker into an O. "Ouch. That's gotta hurt."

"Tank is a prick."

Randy nudges me. "Yeah, but he's our president, so don't be saying shit like that."

Rolling my eyes, I ask, "Can we go now?"

Randy checks his watch. "Yeah, let's go get our weapons."

The Soldiers of War are all lined up like soldiers waiting in a nice, neat line to get their weapons. I walk past all of them to the security guards.

"Can I get my stuff?"

Shotgun taps me on the shoulder, but I don't turn

around. "Toxin, there's a line."

"Only for pussies."

"Well, you should definitely be at the end of the line then."

Looking over my shoulder, his face is anything but friendly. Not wanting to appear scared or intimidated, I blow him a kiss. Shotgun's face flushes red, and he takes a step toward me.

"You don't want to tangle with me, man. Our MC is bigger and badder than yours. Hell, you guys might as well be called the Soldiers of Pansies."

Shotgun takes another step, his face full of rage when a wall of a man steps between us. Craning my neck upward, I notice it's Grim.

He's smiling at me. "Now, Toxin, you need to play nice, or someone is going to teach you a lesson."

Puffing up my chest, I sneer at him. "Well, it won't be you or your little friend."

Grim huffs a laugh at me. "It's a no-violence weekend. Standing behind you is one pissed-off-looking woman, and behind her is her husband. You want to tussle with me, Toxin? We can but not in here and not today."

Sapphire Knight has her hands firmly planted on her hips, and her husband, Jamie, is staring me down.

"What?" I ask.

"Toxin, stop being a dick," Tank says.

My top lip curls as my gaze shifts from the woman to him. "Why?"

Tank's meaty hand lands on my shoulder. "Because I said so. Get to the back of the line."

"Behind these pussies?"

"Don't make me repeat myself," Tank growls out.

Running my tongue across my teeth, I give Tank a chin lift and leave. Shotgun laughs, and I flex my hands into fists to keep control. One day, I'm going to challenge Tank but not today.

Randy falls into step beside me. "You okay?"

"Fucking Tank. Fucking Shotgun. And Grim? Fuck him too."

Randy chuckles and slaps me on the back. "You're okay, Toxin." He does a glance around the area. "I'm going back inside. I want my gun."

"Catch you later, man."

"You're not coming?"

"I will, but I'm going to wait a bit."

"Trying to save face?"

Randy is baiting me. He knows how I feel about Tank. He's the closest I have to a friend in the MC, but the thing with my MC? We're all trying to fuck each other over to get to the top. Randy would rat me out if it meant he could advance further up the ladder. All I need is for him to walk in there and tell Tank I'm talking shit about him, and Tank will exile me or fuck me up.

"Randy, you know I run my mouth, yeah?"

"We all do, brother."

"Yeah, well, I don't mean it." Shrugging, I point at the open doors to the venue. "Come on, we'll go in together."

Randy smirks. "Safety in numbers."

"You got that right."

Sucking in a deep breath, we head inside. The line for our weapons is considerably shorter. Grim has his gun, and he's showing it to Elora.

Won't be long now.

Grim ejects his magazine, checks the gun, and then slams it back into place. Nothing happens. He didn't even flinch.

Fuck.

It didn't work.

Grim frowns and turns his gun over, inspecting it. My heart beats a little faster. *Maybe it did work?* He walks over to a security guard and holds the weapon out. From my position, I can't hear the conversation, but Grim looks pissed. He hands over the gun to the security guard, who picks up a clipboard and flips through pages of information. The security guard looks at the gun, then his paperwork, and shakes his head.

Grim stands over him, his mouth in a hard fixed line, eyes blazing. Whatever the fuck is going on, it's not good. Casually, I stroll toward them.

"Who's put a bug up your ass?"

Grim pins me with a look. "What the fuck did you do, Toxin?"

My mouth drops open in surprise. "What the fuck are you on about?"

"I know you were in this room when the fire alarm sounded." He pokes me in my chest. "Where is *my* gun?" Spittle flies from Grim's lips, his face a mask of fury.

The security guard clears his throat, drawing all of our attention. "He's right, this isn't his gun." He flips up a piece of paper. "It belongs to Tank."

My heart beats faster in my chest as I search the room. I spot Cherry first. She's holding onto Tank's hand, staring at it intently.

Please, God, no, I pray as I move toward him.

Tank puts his hand to his mouth and sucks. This one gesture, and I know I'm too late. The venom is already working its way through his system. Tank looks at the bottom of his gun and shrugs. The security guard walks past me with Grim following. Grim deliberately bumps into me, and I stumble.

It's not going to take them long to figure out what's happened. Everyone knows I don't like Tank or Grim.

I need to run.

Before I can, I slam into Boxer. The fucker is grinning at me, showing off his gold tooth.

"Going somewhere, Toxin?"

"Yeah, I'm going for a piss. Want to hold it for me?" I snarl in his face.

Boxer chuckles and canters his head to the side. "Nah." He points in the direction of the MC presidents. "I think they want to have a word with you."

Sweat coats my forehead, but now isn't the time to panic. If I can get out of this room, I've got half a chance of surviving.

A hand lands on my shoulder—it's Tank. "What did you do?"

"Fucking nothing."

"Why were Grim's and my guns switched?"

"I don't know what the fuck you're talking about."

Tank frowns and looks at his hand, then he puts it to his throat. "Toxin, is there something I should k-know?" His last word comes out hoarse. Tank clears his throat and shakes his head.

"Tank?"

The man steps away from me and places his hands on his knees. "I... I don't feel right. My throat feels weird, tight. It's getting hard to breathe."

"Tank, baby?" Cherry appears beside him, rubbing his back.

Tank holds up a hand to her, and she looks at me.

"What did you do?"

Outwardly, I say, "Fucking nothing." Inwardly, I know Tank is going into anaphylactic shock. It's rare, but there's been a whole lot of research done on Taipan bites, and this isn't uncommon. He has about fifteen minutes before he's dead.

Tank looks up at Cherry, his knees buckle, and he hits the floor.

"Tank," Cherry shrieks as she falls to the floor, her hands on his chest.

He's staring up at the ceiling, gasping for breath, and his face and neck are swelling.

"Someone call nine-one-one," Cherry yells.

Tank's hands fall to his sides, and his eyes roll back in his head.

People swarm around us, and I take a step backward, then another. Glancing around me, I notice all eyes are on Tank. Cherry is leaning over him, her hand on his forehead as she chants his name. Taking another step, I walk into someone, and looking over my shoulder, I'm confronted with Grim's all-encompassing presence.

"You killed your own president," he whispers. "You're going to pay."

"It was *your* gun."

"I'm not known for poisoning people, *Toxin*. I'm a man... I *crush* my enemies."

I raise my fist and slam it into his gut, then hit him in his smug face as hard as I can. Grim grunts but doesn't move. He grabs me by my cut and throws me through the crowd. I trip and land awkwardly on my ass at Tank's feet.

"He's dead," Cherry screams, tears streaming down her face as her eyes bore into mine.

Bearing the weight of her grief, it feels as though the entire room is judging me. Marshal Johnny Saint-Mark pushes through the crowd.

"What's going on?" he demands to know.

"Toxin killed his president," Boxer says.

"No, I fucking didn't!"

The marshal pulls out his gun and aims it at me. "Get up slowly." He looks at those closest to him. "Everyone, move away."

Standing, I look out over the crowd, searching for my MC. My eyes lock with Randy's, but he shakes his head and spits on the floor. This one gesture tells me all I need to know. They think I did this, and I'm as good as dead.

The marshal yanks me through the crowd until we get to a table. He pushes me against it and handcuffs me.

"Johnny, why don't you let his MC handle this?" Grim suggests.

"I'm a lawman, Grim, not a vigilante."

"They'll get him in lockup anyway."

The marshal looks at me and puts his gun away. "What happens in lockup isn't my concern. My job is to bring him in."

"It wasn't me!"

Grim has a smirk on his face, and the marshal is looking at me as though I'm an insect who needs to be squashed.

"Seems like everyone here thinks you did. If you're innocent, the evidence will prove it."

Closing my eyes, I know I'm done for. When they search my home, they're going to find all my beautiful snakes, and it won't take them but a minute to test Tank's blood and see it was a venom that killed him.

Except the venom was meant for Grim, not Tank.

How the hell did the guns get switched?

Elora appears beside Grim. When he puts his arm around her, she smiles.

"It was you," I screech at her.

"Me?" Her hand flies to her chest in mock outrage.

"I don't know how you switched the guns, but it was *you*!"

Elora tells the marshal, "I have photos of Toxin hiding in here when the fire alarms went off."

"Do you now?"

My gaze goes on a swivel between the marshal and Elora. She fucking set me up. My salvation has become my downfall. Instead of occupying Grim's time, she's fucked me over. Elora hands over her cell phone to the marshal and points at some pictures she has on there. The marshal studies them and then cocks an eyebrow at me but says nothing.

"Did you do it?" Rhage, VP for the Defiant Men, asks.

"No."

Rhage searches my eyes for the truth.

"Who else could it have been?" Grim asks.

Cherry stumbles toward us. "Something pricked

his hand. It drew blood when Tank put the magazine back in."

"Where's his gun?" Rhage asks.

The security guard comes forward. "It appears as though Tank's and Grim's guns were switched, I'm guessing so the Defiant Men thought the Warriors of Destruction killed their president. It should have started a war, except Grim noticed his gun wasn't his."

"If only I'd noticed sooner," Grim says.

"No, it was supposed to be you, not Tank," I yell.

Rhage advances toward me, but Marshal Johnny Saint-Mark stands in front of me.

"Out of the way, lawman."

The marshal draws his gun but holds it pointing down beside his leg. "You know I can't do that."

The doors to the venue bust open, and paramedics and police enter. The paramedics go straight to the body. I see them working on Tank, but even if he's alive, there's nothing they can do.

The marshal grabs my arm and yanks me through the room. Members of my MC deliberately walk into me, snarling insults as I'm dragged through the crowd. If I make it out of here, I'm as good as dead in jail. Not only will the Defiant Men put a hit out on me, but so will the Warriors of

Destruction.

Outside, it's daylight, and many of the readers are still here. Everyone eyes me with either disgust, disbelief, or downright anger. It was supposed to be a nonviolent weekend—everyone was supposed to be safe.

"It wasn't supposed to happen like this," I whisper.

Marshal Johnny Saint-Mark puts me in the back of a cruiser, then climbs into the driver's seat. "How was it supposed to happen?"

"It was meant to be Grim. I wanted Grim dead, not Tank."

Another police officer taps on the driver's window, and the marshal winds it down.

"What are we looking for?"

"There's one man down, and you're looking for two guns that apparently got switched. Dust the room and confiscate all weapons. It's a fucking fiasco in there. I'm taking him to the station, but you might want to keep the MCs separate. Most of them don't like each other."

"The paramedics said it looks like anaphylactic shock."

"Seems Toxin here is a bit of a wiz with poisons."

The man bends to look at me. "Not very bright,

killing your own president."

"Fuck you, it wasn't supposed to be Tank!"

"Have you read him his rights?"

The marshal looks at me in the rearview mirror. "Not yet. He was excited and gave a spontaneous confession."

"Best get on top of that, Johnny." He taps the door of the cruiser and walks away.

The marshal starts talking about my right to remain silent, but I drown him out. It's not like I haven't heard it before. This isn't my first dance with the law.

When I see the crowd and the members of the MC who've come out of the room to glare at me, I know it might be my last dance ever.

Elora

Cherry is standing near Tank's body now in a zippered black plastic bag. She looks downtrodden, as though the very life has been sucked out of her. Her red-rimmed eyes lock with mine, and I walk toward her. Instinctively, I wrap her in my arms.

"I'm so sorry, Cherry."

She grips me tightly and says, "I'm free."

Leaning back, I search her face. What I thought was despair isn't. Cherry is relieved.

The VP for the Defiant Men, Rhage, walks over to us. "Cherry, are you okay?"

"Y-yes." She sniffles.

"I could have one of the brothers take you to the clubhouse?"

"No." Rhage looks confused, and Cherry grabs

onto my arm. "It's just... Elora said I could stay with her tonight. There are too many memories back there. I... I need space."

Rhage tilts his head to the side. "You're sure you wouldn't feel safer at home?"

Cherry shakes her head. "No. I need to get away from... everything."

Rhage studies her for a moment, then nods. "Yeah, I get that. Well, if you need anything, you've got my number. Don't hesitate. We take care of our own." He gives her one last searching look, then walks over to his men.

"I guess Rhage is the new president." I look at Cherry. "Does he inherit everything that belonged to Tank?"

In a quiet voice, Cherry says, "If you mean me, no. The deal that was struck was with Tank and him alone. I'll be damned if I set foot in their clubhouse ever again."

"Where will you go?"

Cherry smiles. "Anywhere I damn well want to."

Whitney and I left the book signing together. She's

gone home to change, and I've had another shower. Tonight, I'm going to wear a little black dress. One I hope Grim will like.

A knock at my front door has me throwing on a robe and walking to it. On the other side is Cherry. She bustles in and shuts the door behind her.

"Cherry?"

"Is Grim here?" She looks frazzled. Her normally beautiful red hair is a mess, and there's a mark on her cheek.

"No. What happened?"

Cherry rolls her eyes and throws her hands in the air. "The Defiant Men happened." She walks over to my couch and sits down. "Do you know Viper?" I nod. "Well, he's decided I'm his." She points to her cheek. "And this was his way of making sure I know it."

Sitting beside her, I put a hand on her leg. "What can I do?"

"I need safe passage out of Texas. Grim can do it. Once I hit New York, I can disappear." A tear rolls down her cheek, and she quickly brushes it away.

"Why Grim?"

"He's a good guy for an MC president. He's always been civil toward me. He will know how to get me out unseen."

"Can't you just drive out or take a bus or..."

Cherry shakes her head. "They're looking for me. They have eyes everywhere. If the Warriors offer me protection, I have half a chance at a new life."

"Okay." I stand. "I'm meeting Grim at an after-party for the Motorcycles, Mafia, and Mayhem author signing. It's at a bar in his territory." Cherry smiles up at me. "I'll take you with me, but you're going to have to change."

Cherry stands and hugs me. "Thank you."

"Don't thank me yet." I move out of her embrace. "How about you shower, and when you're done, we'll try to find something in my wardrobe that might fit you?"

Cherry looks down at herself. "The jeans could do with a wash but..." she slides her leather jacket off, "... Viper ripped my shirt."

Cherry shows me the back of her top, which is almost in two pieces.

"Jesus."

Cherry shrugs and faces me. "It could have been worse. Maybe we could wash and dry my jeans? Do you have a machine?"

"Yeah, I do. It's in my bathroom. Come on." I lead us into the small space. "If you want to strip off and put your clothes in to be washed, I'm sure I'll have a shirt to fit you."

"Thank you."

"Well, I'll leave you to it. Towels are on the shelf above the toilet."

Closing the door, I walk into my bedroom, pick up my cell phone, and dial Grim.

"Couldn't wait to hear my voice?" Grim asks with a laugh.

"I have a problem."

"Talk to me." All the humor in his voice disappears with those three words.

"Do you know Cherry? She was Tank's woman."

"Yes."

"She's here. She wants out from the Defiant Men, and she needs your help to do it."

I hear Grim's intake of breath. "Why can't Cherry just leave?"

"Viper is staking a claim."

"Shit. He's their sergeant at arms."

"Grim, she wants out, and I don't think they're going to let her go."

"Elora, I don't want to get in the middle of anything. The Defiant Men are in turmoil right now. One of their own killed their president. I thought Rhage would be the next to take over, but if Viper is claiming Cherry, he could be making a power play.

We don't need the heat, and I don't want to be the club the Defiant Men focus their anger on at the loss of Tank."

"You owe me, Grim. I'm not sorry Tank is dead, and we both know it was because of Toxin, but I had a hand in that, and so did you."

Silence greets me, and I hear muffled voices in the background.

"Grim?"

"Yeah, give me a minute."

It takes him another moment to get back to me.

"Elora?"

"Yes?"

"Bring her tonight. I've got someone who's willing to help. He'll take Cherry wherever she needs to go, but he's not one of us."

"Will she be safe?"

Grim huffs a laugh. "JD is a tough motherfucker. If he says he'll protect her, he will, no matter the cost."

"Thank you."

"See you soon."

Grim

In the space of a day, I've made more concessions for Elora than any other woman in my life. The bar is full of readers, authors, and horny bikers. Red is lusting after any female who'll talk to him, and from the circle of women around him, he is getting laid. The only other MC here is the Soldiers of War. Shotgun is talking and laughing with Goat over near the bar. I'm waiting like a teenager near the door for Elora.

Unfortunately, Marshal Johnny Saint-Mark is the person who walks through the door, and he locks onto me.

"Johnny, what brings you here?"

"That's Marshal to you."

Cocking an eyebrow at him, I cross my arms.

Johnny taps the badge he has proudly fastened to his belt. The air is tense as his eyes stay focused on me.

With a deep, commanding voice, he says, "You don't get it, do you, Grim? It was one weekend of no violence, and now one of your own is dead."

"Tank wasn't one of mine."

"But he was. He was one of you, and one of you killed him. Toxin used snake venom. If that wasn't bad enough, Tank had an allergic reaction, so even if we knew what type of snake it was, he was already dead and didn't know it. It was pure luck it wasn't you. It was your gun. Toxin planned this down to the last detail. He told us how he watched you for weeks as he tried to find a weakness."

"Weeks?"

"Yes."

This is disturbing. To have someone following me for weeks and not have noticed or suspected anything means he may have had help.

Johnny takes off his hat. "This life you live is full of danger, and one day, someone is going to punch your number." The marshal is calm and has conviction in his voice. "The real question is, how did your gun end up in Tank's hand?"

"One of the security guards screwed up."

"Did they, though?"

Elora walks through the door, and I grin at her. "See you, Johnny. My date has arrived."

Relieved I don't have to continue our conversation, I move toward Elora. She's wearing a sexy little black dress that accentuates every curve of her body. It hugs her in all the right places, highlighting her beautiful figure. The six-inch black heels give her a little more height and elongate her legs. I'm captivated by her as she closes the gap between us. It's obvious she feels attractive by the way she's carrying herself, and it makes me want her more. The dress shows just enough skin to be sexy without looking like a whore.

"You look good," she says.

Bending, I kiss her lips. "You look better."

Elora blushes and does a twirl. "You like?"

"Yes, you look beautiful."

Cherry is behind her and clears her throat. My eyes shift from Elora to her.

"Cherry."

"Grim."

"Hey, Grim." Whitney bounds in behind the two women.

"Hey, Whit."

Putting my hands on Elora's shoulders, I say, "I

need to take Cherry out the back and get her on her way. Will you two be okay on your own?"

Elora gives me a quick bob of her head, and I hold out a hand to Cherry. She stares at it for a moment, then puts her hand in mine. Pulling Cherry through the crowd, I stop when I get to Boxer.

"Keep an eye on Elora and Whitney, yeah? Get them a drink."

"Will do, Prez."

He gives Cherry the once-over and moves away from us.

"Where are you taking me?"

"Out the back. I have a friend waiting for you."

"Elora said it was someone called JD?"

"Yep."

Not wanting anyone to overhear our conversation, I keep her walking past the bar, down a hallway, and into a back room. JD is leaning against the far wall. His leather is adorned with patches and pins, but none of them are affiliations for any MC. A deep scar runs from his cheek down his neck, hinting at a life filled with danger and violence. JD carries himself with confidence as if he owns the world around him. He glances at us, his eyes lingering on Cherry. She is a stunner, even though she's wearing a lot of makeup. I assume to cover the mark on her cheek that's peeking through.

"JD, this is Cherry."

He pushes off the wall and walks toward her with his hand outstretched.

Cherry asks me, "Can I trust him?"

"Yes, you can," JD answers.

Cherry shifts her attention to him. "I don't know you."

"And that's the reason you can trust him. JD isn't a member of the Warriors of Destruction, but I trust him with my life."

The only sign he's heard me is the slight lift to one side of his mouth. His eyes never leave Cherry.

"Grim and I go way back to the days when I knew him as Keir. Long before he was the president of the Warriors."

Cherry puts her hand in his. "I'm Cherry." She holds up her other hand. "No, I'm Cheree. Cherry was my club name."

"Pleased to meet you, Cheree."

JD's eyes come to me. "I saw Johnny come in. Is he a problem?"

"Nah, Johnny is kicking over stones and hoping I'll confess to being a mass murderer."

JD chuckles. "I see nothing has changed between

the two of you then?"

Frowning, I say, "Gotten a little worse over time. He finds it necessary to point out my life of crime."

"Sounds like Johnny. Come on, Red, let's get a move on."

"Just like that?" Cherry asks.

"There's an SUV parked out back. JD will take you wherever you need to go, but it has to be now before anyone realizes you're missing. You've had a rough shake, Cherry, but I'm not getting into a war over you. You go now with JD, or you stay and go back to your old life. Those are your choices."

She chews on her bottom lip, then nods. "Will you say goodbye to Elora for me?"

"Of course."

"And Grim? Be good to her. She has a good heart. Elora might look tough, but underneath, she's not."

"Will do." I look at JD. "There's protection in the glove box and some extra cash. If you need something, call."

"I won't." JD grins at me. "See you in a week."

"Take as long as you need."

Cherry shifts from foot to foot as she looks between us. "Thank you," she whispers.

"Don't thank me yet. Wait till you're safe and out of Texas."

After shaking hands with JD, I leave the two of them alone and retrace my steps to the main area, where I find Elora at the bar ordering drinks for her and Whitney. The bartender looks at me. "It's on me." He nods and moves on to the next patron.

"You didn't have to do that."

"Date, remember?" I say into her ear.

"Thanks, Grim," Whitney says, holding up her glass.

Goat walks over and hands me a beer. "Everything good, Prez?"

"Yeah, JD is on his way."

"Cool." Goat tips his head toward Elora. "Seems you got yourself a…" He falters and looks at me.

"I got myself a date, Goat."

A wicked grin spreads across his face, and he winks at me. "A date? Right, right. Well, have a good night, Prez."

Goat wanders away, and I point to a booth in the back of the bar that's being held for me. "How about we get a seat?"

The ladies walk through the crowd of people and slide in around the table.

"Is it normal for you to have your own booth?"

Smiling at Elora, I say, "Yes. They keep this one for us every night. Only Warriors sit here."

Whitney shuffles around the booth to the other side and stands up. "Sorry, Elora, I see Nicole James. I've gotta go talk to her." We watch her walk away.

"Alone at last?"

Elora tilts her head from side to side. "Yeah."

"What does Elora mean?"

A warm smile spreads across her face, and her eyes sparkle as she explains, "Elora means light. It's Greek. My parents chose the name because they wanted me to bring light to the world." She blushes. "I like to think I'm living up to my name in my own way."

Taking a sip of my beer, I smirk at her. "My real name is Keir. It means dark." Elora giggles. "My dad said I lived up to it, and maybe I do."

"How'd you get Grim?"

"Club name." It's a long story and not one for a first date.

Elora puts her hand on my leg under the table, and I cover it with my own.

"You can be the light to my dark."

Elora leans in and licks her red lips. "Well, you can't have one without the other."

In this moment, the crowd disappears, and it's only Elora and me. This is the start of something good, real, and it feels special. Time will tell, but she's right, the light doesn't exist without the dark.

Want more?
The next book in the Clubhouse Women series is:
Men Rule?

OTHER BOOKS TO ENJOY BY
KATHLEEN KELLY

Savage Stalker Book 1
The Savage Angels MC Series

BLURB

Dane Reynolds

President of the Savage Angels MC.
Fierce, strong, and loyal.
He's had his eye on Kat for a while now and has
been waiting for her to come to him, but he's had
enough of waiting.
He's decided it's time to make her his.

Katarina Saunders

Kat to the world, international rock star.
Lead singer for The Grinders.
Until she has an accident that ruins her career and
sends her running into the mountains, away from
everything and everyone.

Man Trouble

Will these two come together?

Or will Kat's *savage stalker* get to her first?

From *USA Today* Bestselling Author Kathleen Kelly.

Savage Fire Book 2
Savage Town Book 3
Savage Lover Book 4
Savage Sacrifice Book 5
Savage Rebel (Novella) Book 6
Savage Lies Book 7
Savage Life Book 8
Savage Christmas (Novella) Book 9
Savage Angels MC Collection Books 1-9

MacKenny Brothers Series
An MC/Band of Brothers Romance

Spark
Spark of Vengeance
Spark of Hope
Spark of Deception

Kathleen Kelly

Spark of Time
Spark of Redemption

Tackling Romance Series
A Sports Romance

Tackling Love
Tackling Life

Standalones

Wraith
Fealty: A Wraith Novel
Cardinal: The Affinity Chronicles Book One
Snake's Revenge: Gritty Devils MC

Check these links for more books from
Author Kathleen Kelly

READER GROUP

Want access to fun, prizes and sneak peeks?
Join my Facebook Reader Group.
https://bit.ly/32X17pv

NEWSLETTER

Want to see what's next?
Sign up for my Newsletter.
http://eepurl.com/-x035

GOODREADS

Add my books to your TBR list
on my Goodreads profile.
http://bit.ly/1xsOGxk

AMAZON

Buy my books from my Amazon profile.
https://amzn.to/2JCUT6q

WEBSITE

https://kathleenkellyauthor.com/

TWITTER

https://twitter.com/kkellyauthor

INSTAGRAM

https://instagram.com/kathleenkellyauthor

EMAIL

kathleenkellyauthor@gmail.com

FACEBOOK

https://bit.ly/36jlaQV

Kathleen Kelly was born in Penrith, NSW, Australia. When she was four, her family moved to Brisbane, QLD, Australia. Although born in NSW, she considers herself a QUEENSLANDER!

She married her childhood sweetheart, and they live in Toowoomba.

Kathleen enjoys writing contemporary romance novels with a little bit of steam. She draws her inspiration from family, friends, and the people around her. She can often be found in cafés writing and observing the locals.

If you have any questions about her novels or would like to ask Kathleen a question, she can be contacted via e-mail:
kathleenkellyauthor@gmail.com, or she can be found on Facebook. She loves to be contacted by those who love her books.